# 30 Seconds

## by

## Chrys Fey

This is a work of fiction. Names, characters, places, and incidents are either the product of the author's imagination or are used fictitiously, and any resemblance to actual persons living or dead, business establishments, events, or locales, is entirely coincidental.

**30 Seconds**

COPYRIGHT © 2014 by Chrys Fey

Cover Art by *Kim Mendoza*

The Wild Rose Press, Inc.
PO Box 708
Adams Basin, NY 14410-0708
Visit us at www.thewildrosepress.com

Publishing History
First Crimson Rose Edition, 2014
Digital ISBN 978-1-62830-474-9
Print ISBN 978-1-5092-2836-2

Published in the United States of America

**She panted with fear.** *What if they see the chest? What if we get caught? What if my breath stinks and I'm breathing right into Officer Hottie's face?* She shut her mouth and let oxygen flow through her nose.

Her eyesight slowly adjusted to the darkness inside the chest and she could see Officer Herro's silhouette. His head was turned and he was listening to the thuds of heavy boots getting louder; the intruders were coming their way.

Then the thunder of footsteps sounded right next to them. "There's no one here, Red," someone announced.

"Look for documents," a man ordered, who Dani could only assume was Red. "I want the name of the person I'm going to kill."

A moment later, there was a reply. "All the mail is addressed to a Dr. Hart."

Hearing her name said aloud by one of the men who had ransacked her place made her want to gasp. Her mouth fell open and her breath was reversing into her lungs, but before she could make a sound, Officer Herro lowered his lips to hers, silencing her.

Stunned, she could only lie beneath him with her eyes wide and her body tense. She couldn't believe he was kissing her. She wanted to push him back, but knew if she did he might hit the inside of the chest, giving away their hiding place. That was when she realized he was kissing her so she wouldn't gasp.

## Dedication

To everyone in the medical field
for their dedication to save lives.

To everyone in law enforcement
for their promise to serve and protect.

To my editor, Lori Graham,
for taking a chance on me
with *Hurricane Crimes* and
helping me to start my career.

And to my good friend,
Danielle Wood, Dani's namesake.

Chapter One

Dani Hart jogged up the five flights of stairs to her small but homey apartment in the heart of Cleveland. Fresh snow soaked the bottom of her scrubs, the soles of her wet sneakers squeaked against the wood, and her white medical coat floated behind her.

After pulling an all-nighter at the E.R., topped with three emergency operations, she couldn't wait to sink into bed with a pint of coffee flavored ice cream. The thought of the frozen dairy stashed in her freezer gave her the extra boost of energy she needed to conquer the last dozen steps. She blindly rounded the curve and rammed head first into a solid chest. Strong hands steadied her before she could tumble down the stairs, and she found herself staring into evergreen eyes.

She gave the man wearing a knit beanie an exhausted smile. She couldn't help but notice how handsome he was and how her stomach fluttered with attraction. "I'm sorry, I wasn't paying attention to where I was going. Are you okay?"

His gaze jumped from the staircase to her; he seemed jittery. "I'm fine. Don't worry about it."

She wasn't worried about it. At that point, all she could think about was digging a giant spoon into her ice cream. She went to take a step back and the man yanked her to his chest. Her eyes widened in surprise.

"Stairs," he told her.

"Oh, right. Excuse me." She slipped past him and bounded up the last steps.

She had the first apartment on the floor, which meant she was closer to her pajamas and cold treat, but she grew impatient while she rummaged through her bag for her keys. Naturally, they were at the bottom. She pulled out a lump of key chains the size of her fist and fiddled for the key with the red dot of nail polish on it. She pushed it into the lock but the door stayed closed. Mumbling an oath, she gave the door a good, hard nudge with her shoulder to dislodge it from the frame. The bang carried throughout the hallway.

She had no time to react when a strong force bowled her through the doorway of her apartment, and a large hand plastered over her mouth. The man she had bumped into on the stairs had a firm grip on her as he kicked the door closed behind them. She struggled to get free, but his hold kept her back pressed against his chest.

"It's okay. I'm a cop. My name is Blake Herro." He hauled her into the living room. "There are six armed men coming up the stairs. We need to hide. Where can we hide?"

Her mind went blank, she even forgot about the ice cream.

"Where?" he demanded with a quick shake.

She pointed to the six-foot long, three-foot high handcrafted cedar chest she used for a coffee table. Officer Herro pulled her to it and flung open the lid.

"Get in," he ordered.

She didn't think twice as she lifted her feet and lay flat on the bottom. He climbed in after her. As soon as the lid lowered, the door to her apartment burst open.

He laid a finger over her lips. She nodded. The inside of the chest was so cramped his back pressed against the inside of the lid, his body crushed hers, their limbs twisted and tangled uncomfortably. At least he braced himself on his forearms to take his weight off her lungs so she could breathe.

"You're positive this is the apartment, Tony?" A man's voice roared.

"The keys are still in the door," another man replied.

From inside the chest, Dani heard her jumble of keys hit the floor.

"Check the damn place," the first man ordered. "And kill anyone you find."

Dani's heart catapulted in her chest. She didn't like being stuck inside her grandmother's chest. It made her feel claustrophobic, and worst, it made her feel like she was in a coffin. She jolted beneath Officer Herro when she heard a loud crash. He cupped her shoulders to keep her still. The six men were breaking anything and everything as they went along with their business.

She panted with fear. *What if they see the chest? What if we get caught? What if my breath stinks and I'm breathing right into Officer Hottie's face?* She shut her mouth and let oxygen flow through her nose.

Her eyesight slowly adjusted to the darkness inside the chest and she could see Officer Herro's silhouette. His head was turned and he was listening to the thuds of heavy boots getting louder; the intruders were coming their way.

Then the thunder of footsteps sounded right next to them. "There's no one here, Red," someone announced.

"Look for documents," a man ordered, who Dani

could only assume was Red. "I want the name of the person I'm going to kill."

A moment later, there was a reply. "All the mail is addressed to a Dr. Hart."

Hearing her name said aloud by one of the men who had ransacked her place made her want to gasp. Her mouth fell open and her breath was reversing into her lungs, but before she could make a sound, Officer Herro lowered his lips to hers, silencing her.

Stunned, she could only lie beneath him with her eyes wide and her body tense. She couldn't believe he was kissing her. She wanted to push him back, but knew if she did he might hit the inside of the chest, giving away their hiding place. That was when she realized he was kissing her so she wouldn't gasp.

She let her body relax. After her initial shock faded, she was able to feel his lips. They were comforting and caused a reaction deep inside her, a reaction that had started when she first laid eyes on him on the stairs. She couldn't stop her lips from reacting to his. It was an innocent connection, a soft touch of lips. Until his hand slid from her shoulder to her neck and the kiss deepened into something else.

She forgot she was inside a chest, hiding from armed men. She forgot she was kissing a cop, and that the situation she was in was dangerous. All of her focus was on his coffee-tainted mouth, and she thought he tasted better than the ice cream in her freezer.

When he eased back, he kept his lips resting against hers. Their breath tickled and warmed each other's lips. His eyes bore into hers as he pulled away, as if he was making sure she wouldn't make a peep, but all she could manage was to keep air circulating in her lungs.

The boots stomping around her apartment headed back toward the door. "The owner will be back, so we'll be back, too," the man known as Red announced.

"What if the doctor doesn't come home?" someone asked.

"Then we'll come for him."

*Him?* Dani thought in confusion. *They think I'm a man?*

Her mouth opened, not from the shock of being mistaken for a man, but because they were running out of oxygen.

"All right, let's get out of here before someone calls the cops and we have to kill a bunch of pigs."

Slowly suffocating, Dani heard the men file out one-by-one and the door close. Officer Herro waited until the echo of hurrying feet grew faint before he shoved the lid open. Cool air swooped inside and she concentrated on swallowing it. She didn't even care that he was straddling her.

He put his hands on either side of her face. "Hey, slow breaths."

She opened her eyes. "I'm fine," she insisted.

"Are you sure?" He looked concerned.

"Yeah, and I'll be even better once I get out of this damned coffin."

When she stepped out, she studied the cedar chest—big enough to fit two people—and made a mental note to thank her grandmother for giving it to her. "It's a good thing I didn't put my medical books in there last weekend," she said aloud.

"Medical books?"

She indicated the three towers of books stacked

beside her TV.

He nodded. "I'd keep this thing empty," he said while closing the chest. "Just in case."

She frowned at him. "What the hell was all that anyway?"

He took a deep breath before explaining. "I've been undercover for a month. Red must've sensed I wasn't one of them because he retaliated tonight. I was able to get away and came in here to hide out. It was early, so I wasn't expecting anyone to come or go."

"And then I came along."

He nodded. "They must've come in right after you, heard you open your door, and thought I was trying to escape. They would've killed you if I hadn't—"

"Attacked me?"

He winced at her choice of words. "More-or-less."

She was starting to get the full picture now. "So they came here for you?"

He nodded.

"But now they think you're Dr. Hart?"

He nodded again.

"And thanks to you, they're going to come after me!"

He grabbed her shoulders and pulled her close. "They will come for Dr. Hart, which is why I need to get you out of here as soon as fucking possible. Pack a bag. I'll get you somewhere safe."

Chapter Two

In a duffel bag, Dani piled in scrubs, jeans, T-shirts, pajamas, underwear and an expensive dress with its original tags because she didn't want it stolen. In a backpack, she stuffed a first aid kit, bathroom toiletries, never-before-worn heels she bought to go with the dress, a pearl necklace given to her by her grandmother, and her most prized possession, her photo album.

When she returned, a black claw restrained her red hair and she wore a pair of jeans and sneakers. Before she left the bathroom, she noted the red lightning bolts of exhaustion lining her blue eyes, but she couldn't do a thing about that.

Officer Herro turned his back on the window. "Are you ready?"

"I don't know," she answered honestly. "This is all happening way too fast." He might've saved her life moments ago, but she wasn't sure if she should trust him. Her mother had always said not to go anywhere with strangers.

"If it doesn't happen fast, you'll find yourself back in that chest."

She eyed it wearily. "I think I'm claustrophobic, but that's not what I meant. What's going to happen now? Where are you going to take me?"

"Protective custody. I already spoke to my police chief and he agrees your protection takes priority."

"Does he know I'm in this mess because of you?" She saw his jaw tighten.

"Yes, he does. Now are you ready?"

"Yes. No. Wait." She hurried over the tile covered in sugar crystals and coffee grounds to the refrigerator. She opened the mini-freezer and took out the pint of ice cream. Even though her life had just been in jeopardy, she couldn't deny her craving. "Do you like coffee-flavored ice cream?"

He grinned. "It's one of my favorites."

"Well, I just might share it with you." On her way back, she saw her keys lying in a heap on the floor. She bent down to pick them up.

"I wouldn't do that."

Her hand stopped a few inches from her keys. "Why not?"

"If you take it, they'll know you were here."

She straightened. "You mean I can't lock up?" She looked at the rack containing her collection of music including John Lennon and Bob Marley records, the case of classic Cadillac models, and original works of art on her walls. All of which miraculously survived the ransacking that caused shattered lamps, a gutted mattress, up-ended furniture, and a broken bathroom mirror.

He looked too. "A squad car can keep an eye on your place," he offered.

She inhaled slowly. "Thanks." Then she remembered the keys for the hospital. "Can I take a few keys off for work?"

He shook his head. "You're going into protective custody. You're not going to be working."

She glared at him. *We'll see about that. At least I*

*have my ID badge in my purse.*

He pointed at the ice cream in her hand. "Do you have everything now?"

She smiled. "Yup."

"Good. Let's go." He opened the window.

She planted her feet. "You've got to be kidding me! Out the window?"

He grabbed her arm and tugged her to the window. "I didn't save your life to get shot to death walking out the front door. We'll go down the fire escape and take the back alley for a couple of blocks." He studied her curiously. "You're not afraid of heights are you?"

She straightened her spine and thrust her chin into the air. "Don't make me laugh." She swung the duffel bag, aiming for his gut. When he grabbed it, she was already climbing out the window. On the last landing, she found the ladder wasn't all the way to the ground.

"I love this part," she claimed as she stepped onto the raised ladder. Before he could stop her, she jumped, putting all her weight on the metal rung. The ladder slide fast and hit the black pavement with a loud clank. With a triumphant laugh, she hopped down and waited for Officer Herro to reach the bottom.

"I started sneaking down fire escapes when I was nine," she told him.

"I'm sure you did."

She glared at him. "Cállate, puerco! Tu eres la razon que estoy en este mierda!"

He lifted a brow. "What was that?"

"Spanish."

"And what did you say?"

"I said it in Spanish because I never would say it to a cop in English."

"What if I knew Spanish?"

She shrugged. "I took a chance. Lucky guess."

"Mmm." He snatched her arm and tugged her along.

They slunk through the alley like stray cats. The air smelled of piss, vomit, and rotting garbage, and it was making Dani lightheaded. She was used to the dizzying scents of bleach and antiseptics suffocating the hospital, but the putrid odor in the alley made her head spin and her stomach churn. She swayed.

"Whoa. What's wrong?" Officer Herro held her shoulder and put a hand to her face. His thumb stroked her cheek. She wondered if he realized it.

"What's the matter?" he said.

She shook her head. "Nothing. I'm fine."

"I'm a cop, remember? I can tell when you're lying."

"I'm a doctor," she countered. "I know when something's wrong with me. We've been in this alley for a while now. The smell is making me dizzy. That's all."

"All right." He took her hand, lead her out of the alley's bowels, and onto the city street. Gas-guzzling buses and air-polluting cars zoomed down the street carrying the businessmen and women doing their butt-crack-of-the morning commute.

Dani and Officer Herro hurried along on the sidewalk. She was wearing a backpack, he was holding a duffel bag, and both of them were peering over their shoulders every ten steps.

"Like we don't look suspicious," she mumbled under her breath.

A few minutes later, they made it to his undercover

car tucked on a side road. He opened the door for her, but she stayed put.

"I'm not getting into any vehicle with you until I have proof you're really a cop."

Sighing, he reached into the center console and held up his badge for her to inspect. Once she was satisfied he was who he claimed to be, she buckled herself into the passenger's seat.

As soon as he started the car, he turned on the radio. "Do you like rock?"

She smiled at him. "My mother gave birth to me at a Kiss concert. What do you think?"

"You're kidding."

"Scout's honor." She held up two fingers. "I was born in the eighties, the time of real rock and roll. Back then, it was all about head-banging and acid, which I've never done by the way."

He looked at her in amusement.

"My mother doesn't like the new generation of rock," she continued. "She makes fun of the piercings in strange places, man-liner, and gothic clothing. To this day, she still tells me my tats are ridiculous."

He raised a brow. "You have tattoos?"

She leaned forward and pulled up her shirt to reveal a string of notes on her lower back. The curving of the symbols was fancy, and the lines separating them were neat.

"What is it?"

"String notes for Led Zeppelin's 'Stairway to Heaven'."

"Good song. Do you have anymore?"

She sat back. "I do," she admitted. "But they are inappropriate to show you, Officer Herro."

"Blake."

"What?"

"Call me, Blake."

"Blake Herro." She listened to the sound of his full name and decided she liked it. "I know Blake is old English, but I don't have a clue about Herro."

"And wouldn't."

She frowned at him. "What do you mean?"

"I changed my last name when I was twenty. It's completely made up."

"Why?"

"My father split the day after I was born. My mother and grandmother raised me. My mother kept his last name but I had no respect for it. On my twentieth birthday, I changed it to a name I could live with."

"And you chose hero. I mean He-are-row." She sent him a teasing smile. "Your future wife and son will be proud to have your name."

He glanced at her. "Thanks."

She smiled. "And when did you decide you wanted to be a police officer?"

"When I was eighteen, I wanted to conquer the world, but I figured I should make the world a better place before I did."

"So you're conquering the crimes in the world." She nodded. "After my accident, I wanted to do the same thing, but instead of killing the bad guys, I wanted to help the injured."

"Accident?"

She hesitated. "Car accident."

"How'd it happen?"

"I don't remember," she answered honestly, but she didn't want Blake to dig any deeper, so she cranked up the volume, effectively putting an end to all conversation.

As she stared out the window, the horrible memories of the car accident that left her in a coma for a year played in her mind. She almost didn't notice the city shrinking in the distance.

She peered over her shoulder as they drove farther away from Cleveland. She turned stiffly and eyed the stretch of road taking her farther and farther away from the police station. Her heart galloped in her chest. Where was he taking her? While she told him revealing stories about her birth and showed him her tattoo, he was driving her out of the city.

She nonchalantly folded her arms across her stomach and continued to sing along with the song as her fingers snuck over to the belt buckle. The door was unlocked. All she had to do was release the buckle and she'd be free.

She may be scared shitless of being in another car accident, but it was better than letting Blake kidnap her.

She eased the buckle out of its trap and held it in her sweaty palm. Blake was driving in the outer lane. She figured she had a chance at escaping without another car running her over. All she had to do was jump and roll.

The song changed and her hand released the buckle. The seat belt flew across her chest and snapped back into place as she launched forward and flung open the door. Her feet were on the edge, her hands braced on the frame. She was flying forward when an arm like an iron bar looped around her waist and pulled her back in. Her hip slammed into the stick shift.

"What the hell is the matter with you?" Blake

demanded. "You really want to jump out of a moving car?" He fought to hold her with one arm and still keep driving while she kicked wildly. "Will you stop?"

"Pull the car over," she shouted.

He swerved the car and stomped on the brake. Her nails tore at his neck, breaking skin. He let out a curse and snatched his arm away, giving her the opportunity to break free. She dove out of the car and was running before her feet even hit the ground.

Her eyes were on the city, an oasis too far away, as her feet pounded the asphalt. She wouldn't make it, not all of those miles, but cars were coming. She was a good runner and she was in great shape. She could run to one of those cars.

She ran as fast as she could, creating a gap between them, but she underestimated the speed of a cop. Blake caught her arm and yanked her out of the way of oncoming traffic. The sudden jerk caused her to lose her balance and she fell to the ground cursing.

Blake tumbled with her.

She fought with him, kicking and punching, but he grabbed her wrists and cemented her hands over her head. "What the hell is wrong with you? I saved your life and now you're running away from me as though I were trying to take it? I'm a fucking cop! A good cop!"

She didn't care. "You said you were taking me to protective custody."

"I am."

"Bullshit! The police station is in the city, not out here."

"Do you want to spend the night behind bars? Because that is the only protection they'll give you at the police station. Is that what you want?"

"No."

"Hey, what's going on over there?" A red pickup truck had stopped on the other side of the road and a black man was coming toward them.

Blake put his badge in the air. "I'm a cop."

The black man didn't stop his pursuit. "Cops do dirty shit these days."

Blake ripped his handcuffs out of his back pocket.

Dani looked at them fearfully. "What are you doing?" she hissed.

He didn't answer. He flipped her over in the dirt, forced her hands behind her back, and handcuffed her. "This is police business," he shouted to the man. "Get back in your truck before I arrest you too."

"You can't do that."

Blake hauled Dani to her feet. "I sure as hell can. You're interfering in an arrest."

The truck driver looked from Blake to Dani. "What'd she do?"

"That doesn't concern—"

"I'll tell you what I did," she cut him off. "I hotwired his car. I didn't know it was an undercover cop car. You have to be careful these days. Pigs drive all sorts of cars now."

"All right." Blake pushed her forward. "Get back in your truck and drive on," he told the truck driver.

With a firm grip, he led Dani back to his car. Both of the doors were wide open. After the red pickup drove by, he turned her to look at him. He had one hand on her arm to hold her still and the other hand planted on the car. He had her cornered.

Apparently, he didn't trust her.

"I played your game," she told him. "Now where

are you taking me?"

"Protective custody." He moved his hand from her arm to her shoulder. "You need to trust me."

"I don't *need* to do anything." She shrugged her shoulder away from his hand.

"I keep people alive every day, and right now, the person I'm trying to keep alive is you. Will you let me?"

She stared into his dark green eyes. They were the eyes of an honest man. She let out a sigh of surrender and nodded.

"Are you going to bolt again, or can I uncuff you?"

"Yes," she growled.

His brow shot up. "Yes you're going to bolt, or yes I can remove the cuffs?"

"You can remove the cuffs." He didn't move. "I won't bolt, I promise." He turned her around and removed the cuffs.

While she rubbed her wrists, he slammed the passenger's door shut and opened the back. "Get in."

"Real trustworthy," she grumbled, but climbed in anyway.

From the back seat, she kept her eyes on Blake, watching every movement. He switched radio stations, turned up the heat, cracked open a window, and took the knit beanie off his head. She bit her bottom lip when she saw his hair; he had curls. She had always had a weakness for curls and his were chestnut with blonde streaks.

*So cute.*

"Where'd you learn to run like that?"

Blake's question caught her off guard. For the last minute, she had been imagining running her fingers through his gorgeous hair. She shook the dangerous thought away.

"I ran track in college for fun. I had to do something between suturing pig's feet and practicing how to administer an IV."

"Is there anything you can't do?"

"I can't whistle."

"Seriously? All you have to do is put your lips together and blow."

She sent him a cool look. "When I do that, I don't create music."

Blake threw his head back and laughed.

Suddenly, she had the urge to rip out those cute little curls. "Did *you* play a sport in college?"

"I didn't go to college. I joined the police force immediately. But I did play football when I was in high school."

"I figured. You have a good tackle." She saw his hands tighten on the wheel and was satisfied that she hit a nerve.

The rest of the way to wherever-in-the-hell-he-was-taking-her was shrouded in complete silence, except for the scream of rock.

*Thank God for rockers.* But when she realized the car was traveling down a snowy road, her hands went cold. She looked about anxiously as she played out dreadful scenarios in her head. A few houses spread far apart on the road. Snow blanketed the roofs and covered the driveways, because all the husbands were still in bed, snug and warm with their wives.

Blake drove the car deeper and deeper until no other houses were in the area.

Her heart punched her chest, like an angry boxer.

*He's taking you down here to kill you.*

*Blake's not a cop. He's one of those lowlifes who pretend to be police officers so they can coax stupid women into their cars to rape and kill them.* And she couldn't believe she was one of those stupid women.

*It was probably all a set up. I bet the men who raided my apartment are his friends. Why, oh, why didn't I put on the defenseless face of a damsel in distress and beg the big, black man for help?*

He pulled the car up a snowy driveway, and she eyed the white house with dark green trim the exact color of Blake's eyes. The house looked inviting as though it wanted to leap off its concrete base and hug her with its shutters, but that didn't stop all the blood from rushing from her face.

"This is your place, isn't it?"

"Yes."

*Oh shit, oh shit, oh shit.*

"But I'd prefer if you'd call it protective custody."

"I am not going in there," she objected and crossed her arms defiantly.

"Well, you can live out your protective custody in my car if you'd prefer, but you'll have to do it without heat." He turned off the engine.

She felt Jack Frost nip her skin instantly. "How long do I have to stay here?"

"Hopefully not long. My boys will be hunting down the men who are—"

"Hunting me?"

He looked at her. "I swear I won't hurt you. I want you to believe that."

She met his eyes. They were demanding but gentle.

He got out of the car and opened the back door, but

she didn't move. Then he took his gun out of its holster.

*This is it. I'm going to die. Or maybe I'll be one of those miraculous cases where the victim gets shot in the head and lives to tell the tale.*

"Here." He put the gun on the seat next to her. "You can hold onto that."

Now that she did not expect. A police officer never gives his gun to a civilian. Never! And yet Blake told her to take his.

"Go on." His eyes told her it was okay. "I don't want you looking at me out of the corner of your eye every minute you're here, so I'm letting you hold on to it for reassurance." He took two steps in retreat. "Take your time."

She scrutinized the gun lying on the beige seat. Outside, Blake rocked on his feet, whistling. The bastard was actually whistling. And what was worse was the fact he was good enough she could recognize the song—"Stairway to Heaven."

Muttering between her teeth, she picked up the gun and slid out. She sent Blake a steely look. "I don't intend on using this," she informed him, "but if I have to, I know how to cut a twelve inch incision with perfect precision."

"Glad to hear, but that's not a scalpel you're holding. That's a gun."

"I know," she growled. "I meant if I have to use this thing I have a steady hand and excellent aim."

"Thanks for the warning."

"It's not a warning. It's a fact."

"Mmm." He walked around her and she followed him to the door reluctantly.

Inside, the air was toasty and smelled like firewood

and musk. The living room was spacious and cozy with a big, white couch and a brick fireplace. The curtains were green, the walls a pretty beige with subtle hints of peach.

Blake went to the fireplace, tossed in a few logs, and started the fire. She sat next to the flames to absorb the warmth.

After a moment, Blake reached out and rubbed his thumb over her cheek. "You have dirt on your cheek," he told her. "I'm sure you'll want to take a shower. I'll show you to the bathroom."

She followed him upstairs to his bedroom. She tried not to look at her surroundings but she noticed the walls were the same color as naked bodies. The rest of the room was just as sensuous. His bed was virginal white, the mahogany headboard had bars, and a mirror was on the opposite wall.

Blake opened the bathroom door and stepped aside. She wandered in. "Oh my gosh!" Her excited statement echoed inside the bathroom.

"Problem?"

"Nope, no, not at all," she said over her shoulder and walked to the bathtub. *Holy cow! An elephant can fit inside this tub!* In the tub, she would be able to fully submerge, lie at the bottom, and make a water angel. She smiled joyously.

"If you need me, I'll be downstairs," he told her and shut the door.

After locking the door, she filled the tub with hot water, not worrying an inch about Blake's water bill, and sank into it. After a moment or two of savoring the feel of the hot water on her exhausted body, she let the water lap over her head and made a few angels with her limbs. Waves licked the rim of the white porcelain and she resurfaced laughing.

Twenty minutes later, she came downstairs in pink velvet sweatpants and a matching hoodie. She had pulled her hair into a wet bun, her cheeks were clean and rosy.

She found Blake in the kitchen. He had slipped out of the black trench coat and was wearing a long sleeved black shirt that hugged his muscles beautifully. She watched him, smiling to herself as he stirred a pot and flipped something in a skillet.

She set his Glock on the stand outside the kitchen and walked in. "Hi."

Blake peered over his shoulder, starring for a fraction too long before he turned to the stove. "No gun?"

"I figured if you wanted to cause me harm, you sure as hell wouldn't be cooking for me."

He shrugged as he continued to stir. "I thought you'd be hungry."

"You thought right. The last time I had something to eat was a bagel at one o'clock this morning."

"Then you're starving."

She chuckled. "I am."

He motioned for her to sit at the table. "I don't know what you like so I made everything I know how to cook." He set a plate on the green placemat in front of her. She looked at it and grinned. He had made a tomato grilled cheese sandwich, homemade mashed potatoes, and spaghetti.

Blake sat across from her with his own plate and looked at her. "Why are you smiling at the food?"

"No reason," she insisted. "It's exactly what I

would've made."

"Is that bad?"

She shook her head. "No. It's good. It looks good." With that said, she dug right into her food. The cheese was gooey, the mashed potatoes were excellent, and the spaghetti tasted like it came from an Italian restaurant. And she ate every last bite. "Those mashed potatoes were fabulous," she claimed.

"My grandmother's recipe. It was the only thing she was able to teach me how to cook. My sister is the chef in the family. That spaghetti sauce was hers."

"She makes her own spaghetti sauce?"

"She uses it in her restaurant and sells it to her customers. She gives me a couple of jars every month."

"Tell your sister she makes the best damn sauce I've ever tasted. And that grilled cheese was also the best I ever had. No lie."

"Well now, I created the grilled cheese on my own." He picked up the plates and set them in the sink. "I'm going to go up and take a shower. The door will be unlocked if you need me."

"Okay." She didn't know why the little detail about the door being unlocked while he was wet and naked had her heart racing.

*Oh, wait, that's why!*

Chapter Three

"Dani...Dani, wake up."

Dani's eyes sprang open and she started to bolt upright, but gentle hands stilled her. "It's okay. It's Officer Herro. Blake." She laid her cheek back on the couch cushion in relief. She wasn't even aware she had fallen asleep.

"Have they come for me?" she asked, her voice drenched with sleep.

"No, you're safe here."

"Then why'd you wake me?"

"I don't want you to sleep on the couch. There's a bed upstairs. I would've carried you but I didn't want you to wake up in my arms and claw me to death."

She nearly laughed except she saw the red marks on his neck. She ran a fingertip down a long, irritated scratch. "I'm sorry."

"Don't be. It was self-defense."

Behind him, she could see the gun where she had left it. He gave it to her so she'd trust him, but also if she ever thought she needed it for protection.

She released a yawn and Blake took her hand. "Come on." She shuffled along beside him and let him usher her up the stairs, a hand on her lower back. Her eyes were drooping when they came to Blake's bedroom. She didn't even know it until she caught a glimpse of the white bed between her falling eyelids.

She turned abruptly.

"Where are you going?" he said.

"To sleep." She started for the door but he shifted in front of her.

"You can sleep in my bed."

She sent him a withering look. "If you think I'm going to tumble into your bed because you saved my life, which has yet to be determined, you'd be smart to think again."

Blake merely lifted a hand. "I'm sleeping on the couch," he answered dryly.

"No," she said. He raised an eyebrow in question. "I don't want to take your bed."

"You're not. I'm letting you."

"We're both adults," she pointed out. "I'm sure we can share the same bed."

Blake shook his head. "I'm a cop. There are rules."

"I don't want to kick you out of your own bed. I was comfortable enough on the couch." She would've slept on the floor; that was how exhausted she was.

"I don't want you sleeping on the couch."

"It's your bed," she shouted stubbornly.

"And I want you in it!" The silence that followed laughed at them. "I don't want you on the damn couch," he finally said.

"Okay. Fine." She sank onto the bed and the white comforter puffed around her. She bounced, testing the firmness of the mattress. "Comfy."

Blake set his gun on the nightstand. "Now go to sleep."

"Yes, sir." She grinned at him when he glared at her. "Goodnight."

"Actually, it's ten in the morning."

"Whatever."

\*\*\*\*

She slept like the dead for the rest of the day. In fact, she slept so well she didn't hear her beeper go off until the sixth urgent attempt. Her hand crawled over to the nightstand toward the beeper and touched the gun. She sat up so fast her heart stopped. After one thoughtless moment, her heart punched her chest and she remembered everything.

She rubbed her tired eyes as the beeper screamed at her again. She picked it up and cursed. It was the E.R. She swung her legs over the edge of the bed and was happy to see Blake had a phone right next to his bed. She picked it up to call the hospital where she worked.

Deanna, her friend and a nurse, answered the other line. "Hey, it's Hart. What's going on?"

"It's about damn time! I've paged you five times. Cory paged you once. Even Norland paged you."

Dani winced. Norland was the Chief of Surgery. Her fellow resident paging her was one thing, but the Chief of Surgery? That was never good!

"What's going on," she repeated.

"There's been a car accident on the freeway. The police don't even know how many cars are involved in the pileup and we're the closest hospital."

"Of course we are."

"You better get here now!" Deanna hung up before Dani could explain she was being detained by a cop and couldn't leave. But a pileup…?

She dialed a taxi service, told them the street name from the stop sign she saw, the numbers on the front of the house, and gave the strict instructions not to honk. She would be outside waiting. She dressed quickly and snuck down stairs on her tiptoes with her breath captive in her lungs. But she couldn't just leave. Blake was a cop and was likely to panic. So she did the reasonable thing and left him a note on the coffee table.

Before she left, she paused by the couch to study Blake while he slept. He wore soft gray flannel pants and a white shirt, the cotton fibers molding his toned body. It was enough to make her want to curl up right next to him, to feel his taut muscles against her.

*You read too many romance novels*, she snapped at herself. *Stop being a romantic.*

She turned her back on her fantasy and, with stealthy moves, made her way to the front door. She looked for signs of an alarm system, and when she didn't see one, she shook her head at Blake's lack of security.

*He calls himself a police officer?* She eased the door open and smiled devilishly when it didn't even creak.

The air outside bit her cheeks, sank its teeth into her neck, and slipped its icy fingers into her hair. She hadn't bothered with a coat other than the white coat that told the world she was a doctor. She made her way through the snow to the edge of the street where she waited for the cab and hopped in place to keep warm. The yellow cab turned onto the street and pulled up to her.

"I'm a doctor," she told the cabby. "There was a huge accident and I need to get to the hospital pronto!" The driver turned the car and sped down the snowy road. "Whoa! Slow down! I don't want to get to the hospital strapped to a gurney."

The cab pulled up to the hospital just ahead of

three ambulances. She threw money at the driver, not caring if she gave him too much, and flew out the door, slamming it behind her. She was at the closest ambulance as the doors to the hospital opened and doctors flooded out.

Dr. Norland saw her immediately. "Right on time. Take the next one, I've got this."

She nodded, skirting around the ambulance as the paramedics lowered the gurney. She glanced at the man strapped to it and saw the giant piece of windshield sticking out of his chest. That type of trauma was Norland's specialty; it was probably in his heart and removing it would cause him to bleed out.

She hurried to the next ambulance. "What do we have?" she asked the paramedics.

"Head injury. She was unconscious when we found her."

Dani looked at the young girl lying on the gurney. She had bright gold hair and clear cerebrospinal fluid was seeping out of her nose. Dani froze because she knew the girl had a serious head injury, as she had when she was eighteen years old, but she wasn't going to let this girl end up in a coma. She grabbed the gurney and rushed her to a trauma room.

She lifted the girl's right eyelid and shone a penlight directly onto her eye. She went to check the other eye when the girl started to convulse violently. She ordered a nurse to give her a dose of anti-seizure medication. After thirty seconds, the convulsions died down.

"I need to do a Craniotomy," she told her team.

The nurses looked startled. "But you don't know what kind of head injury she has. She needs a CT."

"She has bleeding and swelling in the brain. If we don't relieve the pressure now she will go into a deep coma or a vegetative state. I'm opening her skull. If you don't like it get out of my damn trauma room!"

**\*\*\*\***

Four hours later, the E.R. was finally back to its normal chaotic state. The pressure in the young girl's brain had gone down thanks to the window Dani had cut into her skull. She treated dozens of other car accident patients, stitched countless lacerations, and performed intensive surgery. Now she was walking down the sterilized hallway, her clean white coat tapping her legs, her hair tucked beneath a surgical cap. A smile was on her face because when she stepped out of the operating room, Deena told her the girl, Tara, had woken up.

She was on her way to check on Tara when she saw them. Six men were crowding the nurse's desk. One had a long, jet-black ponytail and olive skin. His arm lay across his stomach, his hand hidden beneath his buckskin jacket. She had seen enough movies to know it caressed a gun. Next to him was a man with a thin goatee framing a sinister smile. Another had carpet sideburns. One man towered over all of them and, standing on the edge of the group, was a man with arm muscles as big as her head. In the middle was a man in a long, leather coat with brown hair draped over his forehead.

Dani pressed her back against the wall and peeked around the corner. "I'm looking for a doctor, ma'am," the man in the middle said to the nurse. She recognized his voice instantly. It was the voice of one of the men who broke into her apartment—Red.

"Well, you've come to the right place. Is there a specific doctor you're looking for?"

"Yes, ma'am, I'm looking for Dr. Hart."

"No problem." She picked up her phone. "I'll see if I can find Dr. Hart for you."

Dani retraced her steps and opened the door to the waiting room. She ignored the stares of all the people hoping she would take them into an exam room next for treatment. She made it to the entrance of the waiting room, a few yards past the nurse's desk, and a few yards closer to the hospital's doors. She slipped out, desperately trying to be invisible as she walked toward the doors, but the nurse looked up and saw her.

"Oh." The nurse hung up the phone. "Dr. Hart is right there."

Dani bolted and was out the door instantly. Her feet ate the pavement. With a head start, combined with her long legs and cheetah speed, she was far ahead of them. She flew down the sidewalk; the many pedestrians a blur. Behind her, she could hear the thunder of six pairs of boots as the men ran after her, but she never slowed her pace.

Then a shot rang out. She didn't know where the bullet went, but terrified screams erupted all around her. Some of the people fell to the ground as the rest scrambled into the street with oncoming cars.

When she realized they didn't care about shooting her in broad daylight, she doubled her speed. She dashed across the road, ignoring the blinking red hand that warned all pedestrians not to cross. A blare of a horn forged toward her. It grew louder the closer she got to the sidewalk. She leapt onto the curb a second before a delivery truck plowed by, its horn still screaming. Not even the fear of being hit by a car could slow her down a fraction.

Two more shots rang out. She ducked, losing some momentum, but she quickly straightened her body and forced her legs to go even faster. The wind whipped around her and a curl fell onto her face. She could feel the elastic band of the surgical cap slipping off her head as she blew past cars stuck in traffic.

When another clump of hair fell free, she cursed. The last thing she needed was for the cap to slip off and set loose all of her hair. She eyed a building under construction a few paces ahead and the alley beside it. She whipped around the corner. Once hidden inside the alley, she ripped the cap of her head, yanked her arms out of her white coat, and pulled the scrub top off so all she wore were her blue scrub pants and a long-sleeved shirt. She chucked the clothes into the dumpster nestled in the corner of the alley and jumped over a slimy puddle. When the men entered the alley, she had already slipped inside the building. She slithered through the slabs of concrete, beer cans, piles of wood, and fast food bags. Through the half-completed walls she could hear the beat of twelve heavy boots.

She reached the front door and calmly stepped onto the sidewalk. Even though her leg muscles were yelling, "Go, go, go," she walked as coolly as she could manage with her heart thudding inside her chest.

With a sly peek over her shoulder, she could see the six men running toward the cluster of pedestrians. She inched her way through the mess, her hand trailing along the wall, groping for the corner that was a foot away. Her heart raced faster as she fought to get to the edge of the building. If she could get there, she knew she'd be able to change direction and run before they could see her again.

She snuck through the cramped bodies, trying to blend in because if they saw her scrubs they'd know her identity immediately. She slipped around the last person in her way and slithered like a snake around the corner. As soon as she was out of sight, she broke into a dead run. She figured she could duck inside a shop or dive inside a dumpster, as unappealing as that sounded.

Suddenly, a peal of sirens cut the air and a police car zoomed past. She peered over her shoulder to see the pedestrians streaming across the road, but she couldn't see anyone coming after her. She turned back around and ran right into Blake's arms. He held her tight and she gripped his jacket in her hands as her heart thumped wildly.

"It's okay," he told her. "It's okay." He pulled her back and examined her. "Are you hurt?"

Panting, she shook her head. She was cold and her muscles were quivering, but she was fine.

Blake pulled her back to him, holding her hard against his body as though he wanted her inside him. It felt good to be in his arms, as if nothing could hurt her.

His hands moved up and down her chilled arms to rub away the cold. "Here." He took off his jacket and draped it over her shoulders. "Put this on." She slipped her arms through. The inside was warm from his body. She hugged his jacket around her, wanting his body heat to seep into her skin.

"Can you walk?" He looked at her with concern. "I can carry you."

Her muscles were trembling and her legs were shaking. She would've loved to be carried by Blake, but he would've been carrying her pride too. She smiled and shook her head. "I'm fine." Her declaration didn't stop him from putting his arm around her though.

When they came out onto the street, a cop car pulled up beside them. "Where are they?" Blake wanted to know.

"Hell if I know," the officer answered. "They were heading toward the pedestrians waiting to cross the street. By the time I got there, they were gone. They must've split up in the crowd." He looked at Dani. "Are you all right, Miss?"

"Fine. Thank you."

"My name is Max. I'm Blake's partner." She took the hand he held out to her through the opened window. "You're freezing. You should get in, warm up." Blake opened the door for her.

She smiled at the back of the police car. "Twice in twenty-four hours. I'm on a roll."

They took her to the police station to file a police report. She told them everything that happened from the beginning as she sipped water from a Styrofoam cup.

"And I ran," she said. As a matter of fact, she had run two miles.

"Thank you, Ms. Hart." The officer writing the report nodded to Chief Witten, a built man with cocoa skin and amber eyes, who leaned over the table.

Chief Witten handed her a fat binder. "Now I need you to identify the men you saw in the hospital."

Heaving an exhausted sigh, she flipped the cover and scanned the faces on each page. She forced herself to focus. *Find them,* she ordered herself. *Find them.*

Several pages in, she pointed at a picture. The man's hair wasn't in a ponytail or as long, but it was as black as ever. "He's one of them."

The young officer glanced at Chief Witten and they smiled at each other. "That's Tony London, a man charged with nearly every crime."

Next, she found the man with the goatee, the man with the thick sideburns, the tall man, and the bulky man, but she couldn't find the man who had been standing in the middle of the group. With a few pages left, all the faces were blending into one.

She paused, looked at a picture through squinting eyes, but she couldn't tell. *Damn it*, she couldn't tell. She turned the page. The two men looked at one another. Chief Witten shook his head.

Frowning, she turned the page back and leaned forward for a closer look. "He has brown hair now," she said while starring at a picture of a man with blond hair. "This is the man they call Red."

Chief Witten took the binder from her. "Good job, Ms. Hart."

"Why do they call him Red?" she wondered.

"Because of all the blood on his hands."

She swallowed. "Who is he?"

"He's the leader of a Mob."

All of the blood drained from her face. "I'm sorry, what? Mob? As in a criminal family?"

Chief Witten nodded. "They're not all of blood, but they certainly are family. They aren't after drugs, diamonds, or money though. Their goal is to kill cops." He let out a breath before continuing. "When Red was twelve-years-old, a cop killed his father during a sting operation. At sixteen, he killed his first cop and got away with it. Ever since he's been hell bent on getting vengeance. Last month, he and his men killed ten police officers."

Dani stood abruptly. She was too shocked, too scared to stay seated. She put a hand over her trembling heart to calm it. "I remember," she said, her voice shaking. "Ten officers were brought to my hospital, I was the resident on that night, and they all died. Even the one I fought for five hours to keep alive." She didn't like to lose a life, especially one who died protecting the lives of everyone else. "And Blake went undercover? He pretended to be one of them? Why the hell would anyone do that? He could have been killed!"

"We needed to know which officers they were going to target next," Chief Witten explained. "Blake wanted to do it. He knew the risks."

Dani's head spun. "They believe Blake is Dr. Hart. What if they find out I'm really Dr. Hart and think I'm working with the man who tricked them? They'll want *me* dead too!"

"We won't let that happen, Ms. Hart."

At that moment, Blake stepped into the room. She glanced at him and put a hand to her forehead. She was breathing fast and the room was whirling. She knew the signs, knew what was going to happen. She looked at Blake. "I'm sorry," she said.

Blake made his way to her. "For what?"

"For fainting." Her eyes fluttered, her knees dissolved under her, and darkness descended over her vision.

Chapter Four

Slowly, Dani opened her eyes. For a moment, all she could see was white but as she looked around, the room became clearer. She fully remembered running faster than she had run in her whole life. Her legs still carried the aching memory. She also remembered becoming light-headed after she found out the Mob was after her.

*I've been in a coma, but I've never fainted once.* Her hand lifted to her face and she massaged her nose. "It's not broken," she said aloud, surprised.

Blake turned away from the window. "Why would it be?"

"When you blackout you generally fall forward or backward with gravity," she explained as she eased herself into a sitting position. "I remember the sensation of falling face first."

"You didn't fall," Blake told her. "I caught you."

Her gaze flew to his. "Oh." *A man tells you he caught you when you fainted and you say "oh"? What a moron.*

She cleared her throat. "Well, thanks for making sure I didn't break my nose."

Blake bent over her and ran a finger down the brim of her nose. Then he tilted her chin with his thumb, raising her face a bit before kissing the tip of her nose. "You have a cute nose," he said.

She watched his eyes lower to her lips. She knew he wanted to kiss her by the way he dipped his head, and even though she was aware this was not the time, she wanted to kiss him too. She could also tell, by the way her heart raced in anticipation, that she wouldn't be able to restrain her own urges if he did.

Startling her and pulling her back to the here and now, the door swung open, killing the moment. It was Chief Witten.

"Ms. Hart, I see you're awake. Herro, get her a cup of coffee and take her home." He looked at Dani. "Not many women can go through what you did today. I admire your strength."

Blake handed her a cup of coffee. She took a sip. "Wow! Not as strong as this coffee," she said and downed the hot medicine in one gulp.

"No woman I know can drink the coffee from a police station that fast either. Herro, make sure you give her something for her muscles. After a run like that, you are susceptible to cramps and we sure don't want you to be in pain. We'll get these men, Ms. Hart, I promise." Blake and Chief Witten exchanged nods, confirming the promise.

"Come on." Blake took her hand and helped her up. "Let's go get some grub. Do you like Mickey Dee's?"

"I would be un-American if I didn't." She ate two double cheeseburgers, a large fry, and an apple pie before clonking out in the passenger's seat of his car.

\*\*\*\*

*Dani relived the horrible events of the last twenty-four hours in reverse. She was running backward. Out of the alley. Up the street. Back into the hospital. She undid stitches, unwrapped bandages. She dashed out of the O.R. with Tara on the stretcher all the way to the ambulance where the paramedics loaded her back on, shut the doors, and sped off.*

*Now Blake was pinning her on the ground. They flew into the air, twisting until they were on their feet, and ran backward to the car where she had leapt out of the passenger's seat. The car reversed all the way back to the heart of Cleveland.*

*In rewind, they slunk through the alley. The fire escape flew back up with her on it and she slipped back inside the open window. Then she found herself lying in the chest with Blake on top of her. And time went forward.*

*"The owner will be back," she could hear Red telling his men. "So we'll be back, too."*

*"What if the doctor doesn't come home?" came the same reply.*

*"We'll come for—"*

*Silence…*

*Dani swallowed. What was happening?*

*All of a sudden, the lid of the chest flew open, revealing Blake and Dani. Red sneered at them as he pointed his gun inside the chest. The sound of the bullet was deafening and the blood that splattered on her face was warm.*

*Blake's body became dead weight. Blood poured from his head, soaking her. Dani screamed. Then Red pointed the gun at her and pulled the trigger.*

\*\*\*\*

Dani thrashed violently in Blake's bed. She was kicking, flailing her arms, and screaming on the top of her lungs.

Blake grabbed her. "Dani, wake up." He shook her to pull her out of the nightmare. "You're dreaming."

"Blake?" Tears muffled her voice.

"It's me. You're okay."

She turned in his arms and flung herself about his neck, holding on for dear life. "They found us," she sobbed against his neck. "They opened the chest and killed us."

"No, they didn't. We're both safe and alive."

She held him tighter. "Please don't leave me," she begged. "I don't want to wake up with another nightmare and be alone."

He ran his hand over her hair. "I won't leave you, I promise. I'll stay with you tonight." He fixed the blanket with one hand and pulled it over their legs. He lay down with Dani clutching him.

It was at that moment she started to cry. She could handle the Mob busting into her apartment. She could handle hiding in her grandmother's chest. She could handle running a trillion miles, but that nightmare was too much for her to bear.

"It's okay. I'm here," Blake reminded her. Throughout the rest of the night, he lay beside her, holding and comforting her.

\*\*\*\*

She woke in the morning and felt so cozy and warm she didn't want to get out of bed. She cuddled against the pillow, wanting to savor the comfort until she realized the pillow was Blake's chest.

She slowly eased away. She couldn't believe she snuggled up to him all night long. She wiped the corner of her mouth with the back of her hand. *And drooled on him too!*

She sat up, crossed her legs beneath her, and stared at Blake. He was so handsome. She wanted to lie back down and drool on him some more, but he raised his arms over his head and stretched. She watched his muscles ripple and his shirt rise. She could see the sexy trail of soft hair peeking out from beneath his pants and the muscles of his torso. Her mouth watered.

*I need coffee,* she thought as she rubbed her eyes. Coffee was her one hope to banish the ridiculous ideas in her head.

"Good morning."

She uncovered her eyes. Blake was lying on his back, his hands behind his head. Looking at him, his curly hair unkept, she felt like pouncing on him. Who needs coffee when you can have him for breakfast?

"Back atcha," she said. "And thank you for staying with me last night."

"No problem. You were really scared."

She shrugged. "I couldn't get those men out of my head. Chief Witten told me they were the ones responsible for the deaths of those ten police officers last month. I remember that night vividly. The E.R. had been quiet, which is always a bad sign. I was the only resident on so I took the most critical. They had pumped eight bullets into his chest." She shook her head solemnly, dropped her eyes. "I lost him. I massaged his heart. I did everything I could, but I lost him."

Blake's voice was empathetic but stern when he spoke. "That's not your fault."

"I'm a doctor," she told him. "It was my job to save him. I lost a man who risked his life every single day to protect the people in this city. Ten cops, Blake.

Ten! I fucking hate that."

"So do I. I want to stop them if it's the last thing I do. I just never thought you would get in the middle of it."

She looked at him innocently. "Oops."

"It's my fault." He looked down at his hand. "My fault," he muttered.

She was about to tell him it wasn't his fault, but his head snapped up and he asked, "How do you massage a heart?"

"Make a fist." He curled his fingers into his palm and she linked her fingers around his fist. "The heart has to be between your hands to massage it." She pumped his fist as she had pumped the officer's heart that night. "You have to do it hard enough to pump the blood. However, a heart is a delicate muscle, so you want to be gentle at the same time." She did five more compressions.

When she lifted her eyes, she found Blake's eyes hot on hers. She cleared her throat uneasily, released his hand, and slipped hers between her knees. His gaze followed them, then rose up her legs to the string on her scrubs, and finally to her eyes.

She slid to the edge of the bed, away from his blazing stare. "I want to take a quick shower." Before he could reply, she was stepping into the huge shower, the water on full blast. She lathered her hair with her peach shampoo until a white halo capped her head. Soapy water slid down her back and legs and pooled around her ankles. With conditioner in her hair, she scrubbed her whole body with Blake's loofa and quickly ran a razor over her legs before stepping out. In a towel cocoon, she brushed her teeth and applied a bit of makeup to hide the fatigue etched under her eyes.

She dressed, tied her wet hair into an impatient knot, and started to unpack. She hung up the gorgeous dress, figuring she would probably die before ever getting to wear it, stacked her favorite books on the nightstand, hid her photo album under the bed, and slipped her clothes into the drawer Blake had emptied for her.

Downstairs, she found Blake behind the stove. She smiled at the scene. No man had ever cooked for her, but here Blake was cooking a meal for her for the second time.

"Can I help?"

Blake didn't turn. He pointed at a spatula and indicated the skillet where four pancakes were getting tan. She picked up the skillet, slipped the spatula beneath one of the cakes, and with a flick of her wrist sent it flipping into the air. She held the pan out and expertly caught the pancake.

"Show off," he murmured.

She finished flipping the other pancakes while he scrambled eggs in a hot pan, rolled sausages, and flipped bacon. When the pancakes were done cooking, she put them on the table with a bottle of syrup. "How do you take your coffee?"

"Black."

She poured the coffee and handed one to Blake as they sat at the table. "You know, you've cooked dinner and breakfast for me."

He shrugged. "You have to eat."

She sipped her coffee and examined Blake over the top of her mug. "I want to cook dinner for you tonight." He looked at her, a forked sausage halfway to his mouth. Smiling to herself, she cut a triangle from her stack of pancakes.

"Why?"

"You have to eat." She snapped a crispy piece of bacon in half and took a bite.

"It's against the rules."

"Eating?" She raised a brow at him. "I'm not asking for a date, nor am I going to poison you. I make awesome eggplant parmesan."

"I don't have eggplant," he said, shoveling a forkful of scrambled eggs into his mouth as if that would end all further discussion.

"We can pick one up."

"Excuse me?" He looked at her. "You aren't going anywhere. Not with Red and his men after you."

*Thanks to you,* she thought.

"Correction. They're after us. I highly doubt we'd see them while picking out eggplant, unless they get a craving for cucumbers."

Blake looked at her as though she were nuts. "I'll think about it." He set his plate in the sink. "I'm going to take a shower. I'll be down in five minutes. Don't go anywhere!" She saluted him with her fork, two pancake triangles stuck on the end with a line of syrup dripping off it.

She listened to the shower turn on and the water trickle down the pipes as she ate her eggs. When she finished, she carried her dishes to the sink, snatched up a tall glass, filled it with orange juice, and chugged down every tangy drop. While licking the sweetness from her lips, she faced the small window above the sink.

The snow was sweating beneath the sun's warmth

and two birds were circling each other in a mad frenzy. Smiling, she filled the sink with water and scrubbed the syrup from their breakfast plates. She was humming to herself when she dunked her orange juice glass under the water and watched the birds. The male chased after the female, charming her with his feathers, trying to get her in his nest. *Typical male.* She glanced down at the glass as she washed it. When she looked back up, she let out a gasp and the glass fell from her hands.

A moment later, Blake hurried into the kitchen with a towel slipping lower on his hips. "What happened?"

She turned to him. "No, watch out!" But he kept coming. "There's glass. Your feet!"

He walked over the glass. "Fuck my feet," he said and grabbed her. "Are you okay?" She didn't speak. She stared at him with wide eyes and her mouth open.

"Dani." He shook her. "Talk to me! What happened?"

She shook her head. "Nothing." She pointed over her shoulder at the little kitchen window. "Mailman. I got startled. Soapy hands. The glass fell."

"So you're okay?"

"Yes."

She was better than okay. Her arms were against his bare chest. He was wet from his shower and his skin was dampening her clothes. She could feel his muscles and see every inch of them. Her eyes lowered to the towel hanging tantalizingly low on his hips. Part of her wanted to rip the towel away, jump on the counter, and pull him into her but Blake released her and readjusted the towel.

"I'm sorry for grabbing you."

"Apology not accepted." Her gaze roamed over his nearly naked body then met his. "I'm not sorry, not in the least." In his eyes, she could tell he was having the same debate—should he take her on the counter now or walk away? She hoped his dangerous side was more persuasive than hers was.

"You will be sorry," he replied, his voice low. "If I get glass in my feet."

He went upstairs to put on some clothes as Dani cleaned up the broken glass. She dumped the shards into the wastebasket and shook her head. *I can't believe I have the hots for the man who led the Mob straight to me.* She dived into washing the rest of the dirty dishes, scrubbing vigorously. Her arm ached and her insides were cool by the time she finished.

Blake came back downstairs wearing jeans and a T-shirt, but the look of him half-naked would always be etched in her mind.

"I'm going to the market to get your eggplant," he said as he picked up his car keys.

"Great!" She stood.

"No, you're staying here. Keep the doors locked. Don't open them for anyone. My cell is on speed dial if you need to reach me, and that..." He pointed at the gun on the table, "will be right there. I won't be gone long."

She glared at him. She knew he was ordering her and despised it. "Well, since you're going to the market, you should get olive oil, mozzarella cheese, tomatoes, and basil." He blinked at her. "Make sure the tomatoes are organic and get fresh basil. None of that dried crap."

He lifted a brow. "Anything else?"

"I'll call you if I think of anything."

"Fine, but don't leave this house!"

She lifted her hand. "Do you want to handcuff my wrist to this couch?"

He smirked. "Next time." And he left.

Dani threw herself on the couch. *Is this protective custody or house arrest?* She propped herself up on her elbows and looked around the room. *This place sure is nice for a cop's pay. Empty, but nice. A man only needs a couch, bed, table, and one killer entertainment center.* She grinned. *Look at the size of those speakers!*

She bounced off the couch and examined Blake's entertainment center. She pulled open a drawer, finding an awesome collection of horror movies. Then she found the music including some of her favorites—Pink Floyd, John Lennon, The Eagles, Sex Pistols, The Cure, and The Who. She took out a CD, put it in the player, and cranked up the volume.

She jumped up and down, threw her hands in the air. She was letting loose, letting the music whisk her far away as her body bumped against the air.

An hour later, the speakers in the living room were beating like hearts inside a marathon runner's chest, and Dani was in the middle of it all. She sat cross-legged on a swivel chair as it spun.

Suddenly, a pair of hands caught the armrests, halting the chair's rotation. She flinched, but she kept her eyes shut to fight against the dizziness even when a hand cupped her cheek and lips pressed against hers. Instantly, she knew whose mouth it was and accepted Blake's tongue into her mouth. She dived into the kiss, wanting to put out the fire burning inside her and squash the need before it could grow into something she wouldn't be able to stop.

Blake took her shoulders and lifted her out of the chair. He pulled her to his body and she wrapped her arms about his neck. He deepened the kiss, making her dizzier than when she was spinning in the chair. Her hands slipped under his sweater and up his back. Her hands tingled with the feel of his burning skin. She heard his moan and tasted it on the tip of her tongue. He pulled her closer, and she strained against him with desperation hot in her veins. It throbbed, pounded, and banged inside her screaming body. Her fingers dived into the soft curls atop his head.

After everything that had happened, she needed this. She needed to touch the muscles that made her feel safe, feel him on top of her, in her.

Right when she thought she would get drunk off his lips, he took her arms, put them at her sides, and backed away from her. "I shouldn't have done that," he said.

Her head was spinning. She slowly came down to Earth and the ground slowly stopped moving beneath her feet.

"Why not," she said and opened her eyes, but Blake wasn't there. She lowered to chair as a crack formed in her heart.

\*\*\*\*

Dinner was awkward and uncomfortable. Dani sat across from Blake, frowning into her eggplant parmesan as they ate in silence. The first words they said to each other since the kiss was when Blake told her dinner was good.

"I'll wash the dishes," he offered.

"Thanks," she said and left.

She was reading a book when Blake finished his chore. She turned the page as he entered the living room and kept on reading. She didn't so much as glance up at him.

He sat on the other end of the couch and turned on the news. She turned her head to the other page, but she hadn't comprehended a single word since Blake came into the room. The air started to hum with tension again, making it hard for her to breathe. She closed the book and turned to him. Whatever happened, she wanted to know.

"Blake?" She waited for him to look at her. "I don't know if it was a hallucination or not, so I have to ask." She paused to collect her nerves. "Did you kiss me?"

His jaw tightened. "Yes, I did," he confirmed. "It was real."

"So why'd you walk away as if nothing happened?"

"Because I shouldn't have kissed you."

She stared at him and nodded. "You're probably right." She opened her book again and was about to resume her fake reading when he took the book from her hands. He was right next to her. She could feel his body heat beating against her skin. She didn't look at him.

"I'm supposed to protect you," he told her. "That's my job." She swallowed as the crack in her heart throbbed. "I wanted to kiss you. I want to kiss you right now, but I can't. I'm a police officer and you're a victim in the middle of a dangerous situation. I crossed the line once but I can't do it again."

"Looks like you're in a bit of a dilemma," she

stated.

She stood and calmly took her book out of his hands. Now she did look him in the eye while the crack in her heart widened with each beat. "And don't worry, I won't tell Chief Witten you kissed me, so you can keep your dignity and your career." She turned her back on him and went upstairs.

In Blake's room, she paced back and forth. *How the hell can I let myself develop feelings for him? He's a dedicated police officer and I'm only a victim, a job.* She stopped at the window, stared at the backyard, the light snow, and the woods stretching out for miles. The peaceful scene calmed her.

*Blake is a cop*, she reasoned rationally. *And I am a fool for letting my emotions get the better of me.*

She had read about women falling in love with their captor, but this wasn't Stockholm Syndrome. Blake wasn't her captor; he was her hero. Maybe she did feel gratitude toward him, not love. She could convince herself of that because it made sense. What didn't make sense was falling in love with a man who she met two days ago.

Snow flurries fell from the clouds and danced past the window. She sighed. The sun was setting. Pink, purple and orange colors streaked across the sky. It was slowly turning gray when her cell phone went off, breaking her train of thought.

She pulled it from her pocket. "Dani Hart."

A man chuckled on the other end. "Well, well, well. Who would have guessed Dr. Hart was a woman?" Her blood ran cold in her veins. She recognized the voice of the man named Red. "You're a fast runner, and you're lucky you got away because if I had caught you, I would've tortured you to find out the name of the man who tried to trick me." Her heart stopped beating in her chest. "Mark my words, Dani, I will find out who he is and kill him. Whether or not I kill you is up to you."

The line went dead, but she couldn't pry the phone away from her ear. She stayed where she stood too shocked to move, to blink, or to breathe.

"Dani?" Blake turned her around in his arm. She didn't say anything, just looked at him through wide eyes. "Give me the phone, Dani." She didn't move. He took the phone from her and put it to his ear. "Damn it." He tossed it on the bed and framed her face with his hands.

"Who was it?" he demanded softly. "Who called you?"

Her voice was barely audible when she said, "Red."

## Chapter Five

Two a.m. and Dani was wide-awake with fear. She was sitting up in bed, her knees to her chest and her arms wrapped around her legs. She couldn't sleep so she sat there in the darkness, her gaze flitting around the room. Every noise, every creek made her body tense. She eyed the door then her gaze jumped to the window where moonlight shone through the blinds.

Knowing Blake was downstairs asleep on the couch didn't lessen her anxiety. Red and his men could sneak into the house, slit his throat in his sleep, and then come for her.

*I'm not cut out for this. I'm a doctor for goodness sakes!* She could handle gushing blood, protruding bones, and mangled bodies. She could deal with needles and scalpels, but she could not deal with cop killers and semi-automatic weapons.

Fear rippled down her spine and her skin turned into gooseflesh. Out of the corner of her eye, she saw the door creep open. Her head whipped around with her heart in her throat.

"What are you doing awake?" Blake asked.

She shrugged. "Why are you checking up on me?"

"I do it a few times a night," he admitted.

The claim made her relax. "I'm not a baby you have to make sure is still breathing."

This time Blake shrugged. "It's my job to make

sure you're okay. Are you okay?"

She shook her head. How could she be okay? "I'm not used to being scared for my life."

Blake crossed to her. "You don't have to be. You're safe."

She looked up at him. "What if they find me?"

"They won't."

"But what if they do?"

His eyes became dark and intense. "If they do, I'm here."

"Blake, they know where I live, where I work, my real name, and my cell phone number. Can they track my cell phone?"

"Yes."

She was ready to jump off the bed and get out of there, but Blake's hand on her shoulder kept her still.

"Most cell phones now have GPS technology in them that can be used to track down a phone's location. Cellular systems are also designed to track cell phones by triangulating the signal from a cell phone between two or more towers closest to the phone. And there is the possibility they have the equipment we use in the police force to track down a phone's location, but the phone has to be turned on to transmit continuously. Even if they were tracking your phone, it will only give the general location of where you are. It can't be tracked to my house. I talked to Chief Witten and he said the best thing is to keep you here. I've been allowed to take a week off, but when nothing happens, and nothing will, I'll have to go back to work."

"I heard his voice Blake. He's not going to stop until he finds us."

"Don't think about that now." How could she not?

"Try to go to sleep."

She shook her head like a child afraid of a monster under her bed. "I'm too scared to sleep."

"What if I stayed with you tonight?"

She looked away. She stared at the silvery moonlight pouring through the window. "That's not in your job description," she answered flatly.

"I rewrote my job description," he said and took her into his arms.

She closed her eyes and laid her head in the curve of his shoulder. The feeling of safety wrapped around her and squeezed her tight. As she drifted off to sleep, she heard him say, "Goodnight, Dani."

\*\*\*\*

*She was sitting in the backset of a car, the leather soft and cool on her skin. Her arms were bare, her hair pulled into a stylish knot with a few loose waves falling down her back. She wore a delicate turquoise dress that swished around her ankles. A smile was on her face, a laugh was tickling the back of her throat. She was happy, happier than she had ever been in her life.*

*The car stopped at a red light and she fiddled with her fingers nervously. She couldn't believe what day it was. She was excited and anxious. She closed her eyes. Oh, it was going to be so beautiful. It was going to be wonderful! She took a deep breath and opened her eyes. Yup, she was still there, still on the way to the biggest moment of her teenage life.*

*She looked out the window where a few stars were glistening. The car started moving again as she focused on the North Star and made a wish. She wished for the night to be memorable. Then a bright light caught her eye. She squinted and stared at the glare of headlights*

*zooming toward her. Her eyes widened a split second*
*before the truck plowed into her door.*
\*\*\*\*

Dani jolted awake. That was the first dream she
had about the night of her accident. It was so vivid she
had felt herself sitting in the car, but she still didn't
know where she was going, which aggravated her. She
was so close to figuring it out, but her brain didn't want
her to know. Not yet.

She was a doctor; she understood the brain could
erase traumatic memories it didn't believe you could
handle. She also knew brain trauma could cause you to
suffer from temporary amnesia. But all of her
knowledge didn't stop her from wanting to remember
the year leading up to the accident.

Outside, the sun was already rising. A pale, golden
light came through the window. She peered down at
Blake. He was sound asleep next to her. She slithered
out of bed, tiptoed out of the room, and down the stairs.

An hour later, Blake found her sitting on the porch
steps. She shivered in the cold with a layer of snow on
her lap. Tears wet her face and snowflakes weighed
down her long eyelashes. He pulled her to her feet,
lifted her into his arms, and carried her into his house.
As soon as she was on the couch, he pulled off the
sweater he wore and slipped it over her head. She felt
his body heat caress her skin instantly. She watched
him throw a few logs into the fireplace and start the
fire. Then he came back to her, kneeling at her feet. He
wiped her cold tears away from her cheeks.

"You're a doctor," he said as he took her hands in
his. "Don't you know about hypothermia?"

"Y-y-yes." Her teeth clattered together, obscuring

her speech. She knew hypothermia was a condition when the body's core temperature dropped below the temperature for normal metabolism and body functions. As a person's body heat lowers, they suffer from shivers and mental confusion.

"So why in God's name were you out there?"

"T-trying to aw-waken my m-memories."

"This has nothing to do with Red or his men, does it?"

She shook her head.

"What is it about?" He lifted her hands to his mouth. His lips touched her fingers as he blew hot air onto them.

She fought to control her chattering teeth when she answered. "The c-car accident I w-was in when I was eighteen." His gaze silently probed hers for more. "I was in a c-coma for a y-year. W-when I woke up, I didn't have any r-recollection of the accident or my whole s-senior year. I still d-don't remember where I was g-going or why."

The frown deepened between Blake's brows. "No one ever told you?" She shook her head again.

"My d-doctor said it was because of the t-trauma and my memory would c-come back on its own time. He told my parents that trying to fill in the blanks would be useless, as my brain would dismiss it. S-so we never talked about it." Blake's warm hands were rubbing the feeling back into her arms. "I may not remember it, but the accident h-haunts me. It took four years of my life. The year I don't remember, the year I was in a coma, and the two years I spent recuperating and rebuilding my life."

She paused. "I had a dream, a flashback, like the

memory of that night was t-trying to burst through a thick fog. I've had it before. I can see the moment the truck hits the vehicle I'm in, but this time it was more vivid. I could feel the s-seat and hear my thoughts." Her eyes lifted to his. He was looking at her closely as though he were looking at her for the first time.

"I'm s-sorry." She pulled her hands from his. "You're not a shrink. You don't want to hear this."

"Let me take care of you." He framed her face with his hands. "I want to take care of you."

She stared at him, shocked and amazed.

"Your cheeks are cold." His thumbs stroked her cheeks then his mouth touched her shivering lips and he kissed her.

Her fingers slid up his neck and into the soft curls atop his head. She sighed into his mouth and pulled him closer. He gave her what she needed. Comfort, tenderness, and a promise he probably wasn't aware he was making.

He pulled away from her slowly. She swayed a moment and when she opened her eyes, he was still kneeling in front of her.

"You probably shouldn't have done that," she whispered, because at that moment she realized she was falling in love with him.

Chapter Six

After her body warmed up and she had a cup of coffee, Blake turned on the water in the bathroom, urging her to take a hot bath. She agreed because a bath sounded good, but the hot water was a shock to her chilled skin.

She soaked in the hot water with her eyes closed, her skin tingling, and she thought about Blake. She thought about his calm, evergreen eyes that never showed what he felt inside, except when they were kissing and a fire appeared. His masculine lips and the way he used them on hers. His body, his voice, and his heart.

She sank lower into the tub. *Stop it, stop it, stop it! You can't be in love with him.* But it was too late. She knew she was in love with him.

*It's okay if he doesn't love me back*, she told herself, and at the moment, she believed it.

When she came down stairs, Blake was behind the stove again. She stood at the entrance, smiling. If he weren't a cop, if they could be together, she would walk up to him and wrap her arms around him. She did walk up to him, but she didn't touch him. She peered over his shoulder into the simmering pot.

"You're making soup?"

He nodded. "Chicken noodle soup."

Chicken noodle soup may be the medicine she

needed to revive her soul. She ate two bowls with the gusto of a hungry child.

For the rest of the day, they didn't talk about Red or his men. They didn't mention her breakdown either. She was glad for it. She hated to be vulnerable, hated to be weak. She despised it! She liked being a strong woman, a woman of medicine, a woman who could handle anything, but there were limits to even what a super woman could handle, so she had a lapse. It wouldn't happen again.

Later that night, they watched a horror film as logs crackled in the fireplace and the flames made long, quivering shadows in the corners of the room. She thought it was sweet when he questioned her movie choice, but she reassured him that even after what she had gone through, even after spending hours performing internal surgery, she could still enjoy horror films. She was curled on the couch, a blanket on her lap, and he was next to her. They were sharing the pint of coffee-flavored ice cream. Their spoons clattered together and they fought over the parts that weren't melted as she laughed.

When the movie ended and the credits were scrolling up the TV screen, she couldn't stifle a yawn.

"You should go to sleep," Blake told her.

"Yeah." She tossed the blanket aside, got up. Blake followed her. She took a couple of steps up the stairs then turned. "Blake." He looked up at her. "Thank you for today."

He nodded.

**\*\*\*\***

One week later, she stood at the living room window. Cabin fever was deteriorating her sanity. She had been locked up in Blake's house for days and it was getting to her. She needed to stretch her legs, to breathe fresh air, to see the sky above her, to feel like she wasn't hiding from a police-killing Mob.

During the last seven days, she listened to every song on every rock album, read all her books, and watched every horror movie. Together, they played every card game known to man and asked each other every question beginning with who, what, where, when, why, and how. Boredom weighed heavily on her. She was at the snapping point.

"Damn it, Blake!" She whirled away from the window. "I am going out of my mind. I can't stand being in this damn house for another minute!"

"Then put on your snow boots." What he said didn't register right away. When it did, she wasn't sure she heard him correctly. Surely uptight Mr. Police Officer wasn't going to let her outside, in range of snipers.

She could sense something brewing in the air and she knew Blake could sense it, too. She could see it in his eyes, in his tense always-ready body, and hear it in his strained voice. Red hadn't forgotten about them. He was plotting his next move and anticipating his revenge.

"What?" she asked dumbfounded.

"Put on your snow boots. We're going outside."

She blinked. "Really? You're not toying with my sanity, are you?"

"Yes, really. And no, I'm not."

She looked out the window longingly. "Do you think that's wise?"

He shrugged, and she knew why. At this point,

nothing was wise. "My men are positioned all over the area on the lookout for anyone suspicious. If anyone came down here, I would be notified immediately and my entire task force would surround the house in minutes. Besides, it snowed heavily last night. If anyone wants to get back here, they'd have to walk on foot. So what are you waiting for?" He was already pulling on his jacket.

She sprang into action. *Free, free, I'm going to be free!* She shoved her feet into snow boots, yanked on her jacket, and was outside in a flash. The air was bitter. The cold nipped at her nose and scratched her cheeks like frozen needles. Snow crunched beneath her feet as she waded away from the house. Blake waited for her at the porch and watched her. Her relief to be outside was so strong she stopped in the middle of the driveway and raised her face to the cloudy sky. She sighed and took a deep, cold breath. The sting in her lungs made her feel alive. She hadn't felt alive since the phone call she got from Red.

If the Mob was after you, the last thing you felt was alive. If the Mob was after you, it was only a matter of time before you were as dead as a doorknob. But standing outside in the middle of winter, with the world in a coma, she felt alive.

She jolted, nearly stumbled when something cold and hard hit her butt. She opened her eyes slowly, turned to look at Blake who was innocently dusting snow off his hands. She glared at him. "You did not just throw a snowball at my ass."

He grinned. "Actually, yeah, I did."

Her response was slow and clipped. "You. Are. So. Dead." She shouted the last word as she dove at the snow, scooped up a handful, and chucked it at Blake. It hit him in the shoulder as he raced to get a snowball. He threw it at her, narrowly missing her butt again as she ran for cover.

Behind his unmarked police car, she made a pile of snowballs. She picked one up, crouched behind a tire, and peeked over the car. Snow sprayed her face from a snowball that erupted against the hood. She fell straight back on her butt, sputtering. A few feet away she could hear Blake's laughter.

*So he wants to play dirty.* She loaded her arms with ammo, sprang to her feet, and shot snowballs at Blake like a pro. When one hit him on the side of the face, she ran for it. After shaking the snow out of his ear, he was up and running after her.

She cut along the side of the house, across the backyard, and into the thick woods. She crisscrossed around trees and hunkered behind a bush. The icy arms of winter wrapped around her as she watched Blake. He was following her footprints in the snow. She stayed quiet, fighting the urge to giggle. She hadn't had fun like this since she had beat Blake in three back-to-back games of Monopoly five days ago.

Her eyes were on him as he searched for her. It was a thrill to watch him, to see the way he moved with stealth and caution. She cupped a snowball in her hands and stood behind him, surprised he hadn't heard her. Carefully, she placed a stick in front of her on the snow and slowly lifted her foot, snapping it in half with her boot. Blake spun and she let the snowball fly.

It smacked him in the face and she erupted with laughter. She bent over, clutching her stomach as laughter rolled through her body. All of a sudden, she was flat on her back, pinned beneath Blake.

She looked at him and his eyes were dark. She understood why immediately. "You can kiss me," she whispered. "I won't tell." He traced her lips with his finger until her lips trembled with anticipation. When her mouth parted, he kissed her greedily.

The inside of his mouth was hot and his kiss warmed her entire body. She slipped her hands under his jacket, needing to feel him. The moment her hands touched his skin, they burned. She pulled him closer, melting into him.

She kissed him with urgency. Her tongue probed his mouth, tasting and savoring his strong flavors. Then he changed the angle of the kiss and his mouth became savage, his lips bruising. She answered it by matching his demands with her own. The kiss ignited her needs, tripled them until her body was vibrating.

"Blake." His name was a gasp and he answered it by sliding his hands over her warm flesh and cupping her breasts.

"Elle," he whispered. She was so consumed in the feeling of burning from what he was doing to her that she didn't mind he used a different nickname for Danielle.

She slipped her hands under his shirt and started to undo his belt when Blake spoke again. "No."

She heard that loud and clear. She opened her eyes and reached for him, but he moved out of her reach. "I don't want this."

"You did a second ago." She stood and stared into his eyes. "You'll have to prove it me. Tell me what I felt was all in my imagination."

He put his hands on her shoulders to keep her back.

"You are amazing and gorgeous. I will admit I'm attracted to you, but I should not have acted on it. I am a cop, first and foremost, and I have to protect you. That is all that is between us, and all that will ever be between us. I can't explain my actions, but what happened here was a big mistake. I'm sorry, but it's the truth."

She shoved his hands off her. "As far as I'm concerned, you can take your apologies and shove them!" She blew past him in a storm of fury.

She felt betrayed because she loved the son-of-a-bitch and he had the nerve to tell her what she felt for him was fake. It was not fake! She'd had crushes, affairs, flings; what she felt for him paled in comparison to all of those things. She thought about Blake late at night. Every time she looked into his eyes, her heart would spring in her chest, and when he looked at her, it would become hard to breathe.

It was shocking that she fell in love with him so quickly, but love didn't have a time limit. It could happen upon first sight or years down the road.

She hated Blake for playing with her heart, but her anger didn't stop her from loving him.

****

She woke first thing in the morning. Her eyes were puffy and red. She wanted to pop them out of their eye sockets and scrub them clean. Even more, she wanted this to be over. She wanted to go back home, go back to work, and forget about Blake. If this wasn't over soon, it would take a long time to repair the damage done to her heart.

She decided to take a shower and let the steady spray of hot water wash away the dried tears she could feel on her cheeks. Steam swooped around her as she lathered. The tension slipped off her body and down the drain where she hoped it felt at home in the sewer. She vowed that her heart, no matter how beat up and broken it got, wouldn't end up there.

Blake's words had hurt her, especially given the vicious way he had delivered them.

She stepped out of the shower and wrapped a towel tightly around her body to keep the hope she felt from floating away. In the mirror, she saw her flushed skin and her clear eyes. She nodded. *Screw the damsel in distress look. Screw the effects of a broken heart. This is not over yet!*

She opened the door and froze as a wave of steam flowed over her. Blake was standing in front of her, shirtless. His chestnut curls were in sexy disarray. His eyes drifted lazily down her body, over the swell of her breasts to her legs. Under Blake's hungry eyes, her body grew hot.

He took a step to where she was rooted in place. He put his hand on her wrist and slid his palm up her sleek arm. Her body quivered excitedly. She wanted to say his name, but was too weak to speak. He lifted his other hand, moved it slowly, sensuously, up her arm. He stepped closer and her lips parted. Inviting, ready, wanting.

Time seemed to stand still, even for just that moment. His arms and hands stopped their movement. Looking at her one more time, he moved her aside, stepped into the bathroom, and shut the door in her face.

She stood by the closed bathroom door feeling wounded. She was naked, wet from a shower, and wrapped in a towel, and Blake was still able to deny her. He may look at her with burning lust, but he didn't want to act on it. He was a police officer through and through, from the tips of his lashes to the tips of his toes.

*He could never love me.* She dressed and packed her bags. She couldn't bear to stay there a moment longer. She scribbled a quick note and ran outside to the cab waiting for her.

"Where to?" the driver wanted to know.

"The closest motel." Or cardboard box; she didn't care as long as she wasn't near Blake.

Chapter Seven

In a puff of exhaust, the cab was gone. Dani stood in the snow, staring at the motel stretched out on the sparkling blacktop. In the early morning sun, patches of snow glittered beautifully, but the motel looked like a dwarf's dirty, little house. Heaving a sigh, she hefted her bag and trudged through the melting puddles of snow. A bell dinged, announcing her presence, when she opened the door to the lobby. A teenage boy with black eyeliner around blue eyes sat behind the counter, flipping through a comic book. He wore a name tag on his gothic T-shirt with Seth scribbled in permanent marker.

"Is that the thirty-fourth edition?" Her voice sounded a little loud in the quiet of the room.

The boy looked up. "How did you know?"

"Because it's one of my favorites. When I was in high school, comics were all I ever read. My all-time favorites are Japanese female super heroes. The illustrations are amazing. I still buy comics when a good one comes out." She shrugged. "I can't help myself."

They discussed comics for a good ten minutes and she realized how nice it was talking to someone different for a change. Someone who didn't look at her like he wanted to make love to her in one moment then push her far away the next.

"Jeez. We've been talking about comics and I totally forgot about my job." Seth smiled sheepishly.

"Oh, don't worry about it." She hefted her bag from the floor. "I was having fun."

"Well, I guess I should ask…are you checking in?" She smiled, opened her mouth to answer, but the rattle of bells interrupted her.

"No, she isn't!" The door slammed behind Blake. In the next second, he was at her side, gripping her arm.

"What's going on?" Seth said.

Blake flashed his badge. "Don't worry about it." He grabbed her bag from off the counter and forced her out the door with a bruising grip. Once they were outside, he released her arm and swung around, but she shoved him back a full step, catching him off guard.

"What the hell is wrong with you?" She pushed him again. "You made me look like a criminal!" She gave him another hard shove.

"Will you stop?" he said, his own temper growing.

"No!" She went to shove him again, but he caught her wrists and backed her into the brick wall, pinning her arms against his solid chest. "Let go of me," she growled.

"No," he shot back.

"Damn you, Blake."

"Watch what you say to me."

Her eyes flashed dangerously. "Damn. You," she seethed.

He clenched his teeth. "You left me a fucking note and came to the first motel you found. Don't you realize Red can easily find you here and kill you?" His hands tightened on her shoulders then relaxed. His voice was softer when he spoke again. "Why'd you leave?"

"Because I wanted to."

He shook his head. "That's not good enough."

"Because I had to," she shouted. "Damn it, Blake, I love you. I've loved you since you made me that damned grilled cheese sandwich. I can't be near you anymore knowing my feelings mean nothing to you, that there will never be anything between us, that the love I feel for you is worthless. It took me thirty seconds to fall in love with you, and it only took thirty seconds for me to realize you didn't love me back!"

"The hell I don't!" He pulled her to him and took her mouth with a hunger that made her head whirl. As much as she wanted to sink into his demands, she pushed him back again.

"You can't say that and kiss me," she told him. "Please don't play with my feelings anymore."

Cupping her face in his hands, all the harshness was gone. "Look into my eyes."

She couldn't resist bringing her gaze up to meet his. Looking deep within him, hope began to fill her.

"I love you, Dani. I've loved you from the moment you ran into my arms on the street corner. I fought against it, but I was in a losing battle. Every time I kissed you, it was exactly what I wanted. I hated myself after what I said to you yesterday. It was all a lie. I love you and I don't want you to ever leave me again."

She threw her arms around him and crushed her lips to his. Her hands went on a frenzy to touch hot skin as they pushed and pulled each other to the car. When Blake grabbed her and lifted her at the hips, she locked her legs around him and deepened the kiss.

He pressed her against the middle of the door,

unzipped her jacket, and slipped his hands under her shirt, touching her hot skin. His hands molded over her breasts and his mouth trailed kisses over her neck and collarbone. She sighed in longing, arching against him.

Feeling movement between her legs, she pulled back just a bit and grinned. "I think we need to get home. Now."

He rocked his hips, pressing his manhood into her. "I think you're right." But he didn't move away from her. He lowered his mouth and began to suck on the sensitive spot just below her ear. All the while, his hips were rocking, intensifying the need within her.

She moved her hands to his hips and increased the speed of his movements. Her head fell back and she let out a moan. "Blake…" She tried very hard not to beg.

The electricity between them urged Blake to find his keys. He struggled to unlock the door. When it opened, he set Dani on her feet.

"Get in," he told her, his voice deep with desire.

She scrambled into the car and he moved to the driver's side. As soon as he took the seat, they were attacking each other again. "I have to drive," he said with a groan.

"Drive quickly." She put her hands on either side of his face. "But don't get in a car accident."

He controlled the steering wheel with a death grip as Dani sucked on his earlobe. He swerved past the curve and sped down the snowy lane to the lonely street his house lived on.

When she unbuttoned his pants, pulled down the zipper, and wrapped her hand around him, his foot slammed on the gas pedal urgently. He was hot and hard. She stroked him, causing him to moan, and her blood to simmer.

He whipped the wheel sharply. The car shot up the driveway. Jolting to a sharp stop, he shoved the car into park and looped his arms around her.

Dani laughed.

"You think that's funny?" He nipped her bottom lip as his fingers worked to unbutton her pants. "Damn it, I can't wait." He took a condom from his wallet, rolled it on, and tore her underwear away while fighting to get closer to her in the cramped car.

She put her hand on his shoulder and pushed him back into his seat. "Neither can I," she whispered. "You might want to move your seat back."

He grabbed the lever under his seat and pulled it up. His seat slid back and she straddled him. With their eyes locked, she lowered onto his body. She purposefully went slowly so she could feel every centimeter of him as he went deeper and deeper inside her. She also wanted him to feel every inch of the space he filled.

She moved leisurely at first, letting the sensation build. When it became too unbearable, she moved faster until they were moving together in a flurry of moans and groans and gasps. She grasped his shoulders, sinking lower, moving quicker as he lifted higher, thrusting deeper.

Her moan filled the car and she leapt off the cliff of ecstasy with Blake.

Minutes later, she shuddered against him. She didn't have the strength to move. She probably wouldn't be able to walk for a week. When she could manage to speak, she said, "I'm sorry."

"For what?" He whispered in her ear.

"For *that*."

"No." He pulled her back, looked into her eyes. "Don't ever be sorry for that."

"It was—"

"Amazing. I wanted you as badly as you wanted me. We weren't going to get out of this car, and I knew it the moment I unlocked the door." He touched her lips with his. "Baby, I love you." He deepened the kiss. Her hands slid up and down his chest, his hands caressed her naked legs.

After a moment of tangled tongues and caresses, she felt him harden inside her. She pulled back with a smile. "Again?"

"Again and again," he said. "But not in my car."

"No." She stared into his eyes. "I want to make love with you in your bed."

She pulled away from him and slid into the passenger's seat. As he zipped his pants, she tied her jacket around her waist and zipped it up, creating a makeshift skirt. She opened the car door and slipped out. The cold wind slithered between her legs, but nothing could cool her insides. She was about to make a dash for the door when Blake swept her up and took the steps in one giant leap. He carried her up the stairs to his room, laid her gently on his bed, and settled on top of her.

"Now it's my turn," he whispered in her ear. He pulled the sleeves to her jacket away from her waist and slid the zipper down, exposing her inch by inch, and revealing the small peace sign above her bikini line.

His fingers stroked her warm, wet flesh sending electricity shooting up her body. He dipped his fingers inside her, rubbed her soft interior. She rode the wave of pleasure until she could hold back no longer.

He took her mouth as his hands roamed over her body, starting a fire on her skin. When she groaned impatiently, she felt him slip inside her, as slowly as she had moved over him in the car. She thought she would go unconscious from the pleasure he created, but she came like a gunshot.

**\*\*\*\***

She slept as though she were in a coma, waking only when she felt Blake's lips press against hers. "Mmm." She welcomed the kiss.

"You're so beautiful."

She smiled groggily, opened her eyes, and frowned. He had on his uniform.

"I have to go to work," he explained. "There will be a police car posted outside at all times while I'm gone."

"What time is it?"

"Twelve."

"Midnight twelve or noon twelve?"

He smiled down at her. "Noon."

"When do you get off?"

"Nine." He pinched her chin. "Don't worry. I'll be back before you know it."

"You better."

He gave her a long kiss. "Stay in bed where it's warm."

"Yes, sir." She winked at him. "Have I ever told you how sexy you are in your uniform?"

"No."

She eyed him up and down. "Well, you are."

"Don't look at me like that right now 'cuz I'd be tempted to stay. But do me a favor?" She nodded as he continued, "Keep that thought for when I return." He planted a quick kiss on her lips and retreated.

Lying in bed, she listened to his boots on the stairs, to the door close, and to the dead bolt slide into place.

## Chapter Eight

She was starving when she came down stairs after her shower. She fixed herself a hotdog topped with the works and a can of tomato soup with a spoonful of sour cream in the middle of the bowl. Full and content, she settled cross-legged on the couch with a tall, steaming cup of coffee and flipped through the channels. She grumbled. All that was on, at that time of day, were soap operas, talk shows, or game shows. None of them really appealed to her but she wanted to help the time pass. After a couple of flips through the channels, she settled on a popular soap with a ridiculously unrealistic storyline. In spite of herself, it consumed her attention in no time.

A psycho had kidnapped a pretty girl and her hot boyfriend was coming to save her. The minutes were winding down and her boyfriend was so close to where the kidnapper had stashed her. Dani was on the edge of her seat when breaking news interrupted the show with five minutes left to the end.

"Son-of-a—"

"We have interrupted your regularly scheduled programming," the reporter announced.

"No kidding," she muttered angrily. Now she wouldn't know if the boyfriend got there in time.

"Gunshots have been fired inside the Cleveland Police Station."

She stopped in the act of switching off the TV. "We're going to Leslie Donald who is at the scene." Her heart slowed when the image changed and she could see the police station. A dozen police cars were jammed in front of the building, their lights flashing. The doors to the police cars were open and officers huddled behind them with their guns drawn.

"Leslie, what is happening?"

"A group of twenty or so men stormed a Cleveland Police Station after one o'clock this afternoon with semi-automatic weapons, shot guns, and AK47s. There have been two explosions inside the building, possibly from grenades or other handheld devices. Many police officers were inside the building when the attack started, including the Chief of Police, Jackson Witten. The situation has been going on for over thirty minutes and it doesn't seem to be letting up. Even now, you can hear multiple gunshots being fired. We don't know yet if there have been any casualties"

"Who are these men?" the anchor at the news station asked.

"It has been confirmed that the men who stormed the police station are the ones responsible for killing ten police officers back in December."

Dani's heart stopped. *No, no, no.*

She watched the live feed, barely breathing. The gunfire never ceased, but every few minutes, it magnified as though a hundred guns were going off at once. A second S.W.A.T truck from a neighboring precinct arrived and heavily-suited men erupted from the back. Emergency vehicles were on standby.

She sat in front of the TV, fear pumping through her like a drug, and her hands clamped around the remote because she was too afraid to let go of it.

*Maybe he's not inside. Maybe he got stuck in traffic on the way to work. Maybe he was patrolling the streets when they attacked the station.*

So many maybes…

She continued to watch as police officers from neighboring cities joined the chaos. They surrounded the building, stood beside their fellow men and women in arms, but no one went inside to help the officers fighting for their lives. They were waiting for the battle to end, for the shooters to come out. By then, it would be too late to help the officers inside.

"We just got confirmation of the police officers who are inside the police station." The footage went back to the newsroom where a man and woman sat behind a glossy table. "Dominique Anderson, Phillip Bane, David Briggs, Steven Corbin, Jonathon Dane, Vincent Evers, Thomas Farris, Blake Herro—"

When she heard his name, the walls around her caved in, burying her alive. She couldn't even hear the names of the other officers. All she could hear was his name over and over again in her head. She stamped her hand over her mouth to stop a cry from flying free.

In thirty seconds, her life had flipped upside down.

*I didn't confess my love to him to lose him now! I don't want one night with him, I want hundreds. God, please protect him. Keep him safe. Bring him home to me!*

"We're being told S.W.A.T. is moving in."

She hugged the remote to her chest when the live chopper feed came on and she saw a group of S.W.A.T approach the front door. They stood there, hunched behind their shields. Seconds later, they scrambled back to take cover. Then the front door blew up and they ran inside. The blaze of gunfire grew louder. She held her breath.

"Please get Blake out safely, get them all out of there safely." She couldn't help but cry out to the walls around her.

All of a sudden, a blast blew out the front windows of the building. Flames rolled out of the empty windowpanes and screams filled the air. She watched in horror as the police officers surrounding the building lifted into the air. The camera for the station she was watching shook violently and fell to the ground. Static erupted over the screen before it turned black.

She grabbed the sides of the TV. "No!"

The stricken reporters who were safe behind their news desk blinked into the camera lens. "We are sorry, but we have lost footage. We will work to re-establish communication with our team on location and get back to you."

"Ah!" She collapsed onto the floor, feeling helpless and sick. She clutched her hands over her heart. Her body vibrated in terror as endless sobs broke from her body.

A moment later, she dragged herself off the ground, sought another channel with live footage, and watched the jittery feed from the camera in the chopper hovering above the scene. The shooting had spread into the parking lot where the mobsters were making a stand; snipers were taking them out left and right. Police officers were crowded behind cars, trees, and walls and were shooting for their lives.

At six o'clock, the news anchors at the station reported that two out of the twenty something assailants were still alive. The odds were against them, but they weren't giving up. The camera in the chopper zoomed in on one of the men as he took out a grenade, but a sniper shot him before he could pull the pin. Only one remained then and he refused to die. He shot two S.W.A.T members and three police officers before he was finally gunned down. By eight o'clock, the death toll had mounted to forty-seven and was climbing.

Not feeling safe enough to venture out of Blake's house, she called her hospital, demanding to know if a police officer by the name of Blake Herro was there. If he was, they didn't know. Many police officers had been brought in, but names hadn't been processed on all of them yet. She hung up the phone and turned to the TV only to hear the names of the fallen officers weren't being released yet.

Minutes crawled by. She paced back and forth, waiting for nine o'clock to come. When it did, she held her breath for a whole half hour. One minute past nine-thirty, a tear rolled down her cheek. Blake would've been home.

She sat on the couch as fear took its toll on her body. She hadn't done anything but worry and pray since the news had first broken. She hadn't eaten, gone to the bathroom, or taken a moment to breathe. She fell asleep when her exhaustion became too much.

Hours later, a sound snapped her awake. Lying in the darkness, she could have sworn she had heard the front door close. She sat up slowly, her hand on Blake's gun, and eyed the hallway. Was Red coming for her now? Would she even care if he wanted to kill her?

She pushed to her feet and lifted the gun as the sound of someone approaching grew closer. Then a dark figure stepped into view. She had to blink to see clearly. When she could see, her mouth dropped. She tossed the gun on the couch and threw herself at Blake. They kissed urgently.

"I was so scared," she said as she smothered his face in kisses. "Oh God, Blake." She looked into his eyes. "I thought you were dead. I thought they got you."

He shook his head. "You have me." He held her tightly. "When I was trapped in the station with guns going off all around me, my men dying left and right, I told myself I was coming home to you and no one, not even Red, was going to stop me. I love you, Dani."

Her heart skipped a beat. "I love you, too." She pulled him to her, demanding his lips while her shaky fingers unbuttoned his black uniform. She paused at the Kevlar vest. Tears welled in her eyes. She tugged at the vest. "Take it off."

He ripped off the Velcro and dropped the heavy vest on the floor. He took her into his arms and covered her mouth. She clutched his white T-shirt. With her hands still shaking, she pulled the shirt over his head. Her palms slid up his abs, down his back, and took his hands.

"Come here." She pulled him to the fireplace and tugged him to the floor. She trailed hot, greedy kisses down his chest, whispering, "I'm going to savor every second with you."

## Chapter Nine

All the exhaustion from yesterday kept Dani asleep for hours after Blake left to return to the police station. She didn't want him to go back, but understood why he needed to be there.

When the phone rang, yanking her out of her sleep, panic settled in. What if something happened at the police station while she was asleep? She answered it with her heart banging in her throat.

"Hello."

No reply.

"Hello?"

When the other end stayed silent, she yanked the phone from her ear and slammed it down. She sprang out of the bed, wrapping the white comforter around her naked body, and hugged herself in reassurance. The phone rang again. She spun about, eyeing it with big, frightened eyes. She stepped slowly toward it as though it were a ticking bomb. She lifted the receiver, her hand shaking.

"Hello?"

"Hey, beautiful."

She closed her eyes. "Blake, it's you."

"Of course it is. I'm calling to check up on you."

She smiled. "That's very thoughtful. I just woke up." She paused. "How are things at the police station?"

"It's a disaster. Red's men killed a lot of officers

yesterday. All the police departments in Cleveland are on high alert."

"Can you do me a favor?" she said.

"Anything for you."

"Stay safe." It wasn't a request, it was a demand.

"I will. I promise."

She took his promise and held it to her heart.

"I have to go," he told her. "I'll be back around seven-thirty. I love you."

"I love you, too. Bye." She hung up the phone with a smile and got up to take a long, hot shower to melt away the stress from the previous day. After she changed into a sweater and jeans, she made herself some pancakes and a giant cup of hot chocolate to enjoy on the couch in front of the fireplace. She felt good. For the first time since the Mob exploded into her apartment, everything felt okay.

She spent the rest of the day trying to find something to do as she anxiously waited for Blake to return. She missed being at the hospital, yearned for the chaos of the E.R. She still wondered about Tara, the girl who had been in the terrible car accident.

To keep busy, and to keep her mind off Blake and Tara, she did what any woman would do. She dusted, polished, and swept to loud rock music. When the whole place was spotless, she baked cookies.

Hours later, as the sun dipped from the sky, she roamed restlessly from room to room. That was how she found an office at the top of the stairs which she had always assumed was a storage closet.

She scanned the books on a mahogany bookcase. Most of the titles were of crime novels and thrillers. She even spotted a few supernatural thrillers about a god and an angel. She took one off the shelf and flipped through it with a smile. She hadn't expected this to be a part of his reading collection. She slipped it back into place and continued to roam.

She looked at the pictures scattered around the room. One was of him as a rookie, clean-shaven and proud. She moved to the desk positioned in front of the window, looked down at the book spread out in front of the laptop, and grinned when she realized it was a yearbook. The heading on the two-page spread indicated the pictures were of the senior class. She picked it up.

"Where are you, Blake?"

She ran her finger down the list of names on the left and paused when she saw the name Blake Junior Harding. He had the same cute curls and blue eyes. "Gosh, you look like a heartbreaker," she said to his smiling portrait. "I bet all these girls had a major crush on you." Her gaze moved over the two pages, over the many faces of pretty girls, to the corner of the right page. A note was written there in a girl's handwriting.

"Blake," she read aloud, "you didn't even have to ask. I wouldn't want to go to the prom with anyone but you. Love, Elle." The second she read the name, she stopped breathing. Her mind flashed back to the moment in the woods after their snowball fight when he had called her Elle.

With her heart thumping, she looked at the names. Her eyes widened when she saw her name in print. "Oh my gosh," she gasped. Her eyes fastened onto the picture of herself at eighteen, her red hair rolling over her shoulders like ocean waves. She looked from her picture to Blake's, her eyes misting. Suddenly, pain shot through her skull and she was whiplashed into the past. She was eighteen again. *Insecure, young, and totally in love.*

****

*Arms encircled her as she closed her locker. She smiled, turned in the embrace, and wrapped her arms around Blake's neck. He was wearing a Letterman jacket and was handsomely young.*

*"Hey, you," she said. "I can't wait for our date tonight. This'll sound very girly, but I've been dreaming about prom ever since I was twelve."*

*Blake kissed her lightly on the lips. "Without sounding too cheesy, it's going to be magical."*

*"Going with you makes it magical," she admitted.*

*Blake pressed his lips to the back of her hand. "Tonight a chariot is going to pick you up and bring you to the ball. Like Cinderella."*

*A big smile bloomed on her face. "I can't wait to dance with you all night long."*

*The memory transformed and now she was in her childhood bedroom with the pale-yellow walls and a purple bed. She was sitting in front of her vanity and her heart was racing. She had waited for this night for so long. She may be the fastest track runner in the whole county and she may prefer to wear jeans and sneakers, but she had dreamed about wearing a glamorous dress and slow dancing with Blake beneath a glittering disco ball.*

*"Danielle, come quick," her younger sister shouted. "You have to see what pulled up in front of the house."*

*Curious, Dani left her room. When she stepped into the living room, three gasps hit her at once—one from her mother, one from her father, and one from Ashlynn, who had been staring out the window. She twirled for them, receiving applause and words of praise.*

*"Come here," Ashlynn beckoned her to the window. "You have to see this. He sent you a limo!"*

*Dani's jaw dropped. Sure enough, a black limo was out front. When she told Blake she wanted a Cinderella experience, he promised she'd have one. The limo was her carriage and it was going to whisk her to the ball where Prince Blake would be waiting for her.*

*"Come on, Danielle," her mom called. "I want to get a picture of you outside."*

*She walked carefully across the lawn, trying to keep her heels from digging into the grass. She stood in front of an oak tree and smiled so her mom could take a picture of her, to document this monumental moment of her adolescent life.*

*After she hugged everyone, she slipped into the back of the limo. She fiddled with her fingers nervously, thinking about Blake, and saw the semi seconds before it slammed into the limo.*

\*\*\*\*

Pain shot through every bone and muscle in her body as she was jerked back to the present. The yearbook fell out of her hands and hit the desk with a loud bang. She clamped her hand over her mouth as tears flowed from her eyes.

"Everyone called you Elle in high school."

Dani's head jerked up. Blake was standing in the doorway wearing his uniform and his utility belt. "I thought your name and hair was a coincidence then I started to piece it together after you told me about the car accident. I didn't want to believe it but…" He glanced down at the yearbook. "It's hard to deny it when the evidence is right there."

He stepped closer to her. "Dani…" He reached out to her, took her arms, and rubbed them. "We met in twelfth grade English class and started dating in October."

She closed her eyes, squeezing out fat tears, and drew in a shaky breath, "I remember everything. Everything I had forgotten about my senior year, prom night…" She opened her eyes and looked deep into his hopeful gaze. "You. I remember you. I remember the first movie we saw together was a horror film. I remember our first kiss was in your car. I remember I gave you my virginity and you were so sweet and thoughtful the whole time. I remember prom night, and being so nervous as the limo brought me to you."

"Being a doctor, I don't believe in miracles as a rule. Sometimes I don't even believe in fate, but this is both."

Blake kissed the top of her head. "Yes, it is," he agreed.

"I have something for you from that night. Stay here." She hurried into the bedroom and reached under the bed. "My mother took this picture of me before I left. I had completely forgotten about it," she told him when she came back and held out the old photo.

He took it. "You were gorgeous."

"You can have it."

"Thank you."

"And since we never got to dance at the prom." She turned on the radio. A rock ballad was playing. "Now we can finally have our dance."

Blake set the photo down, took off his utility belt, and draped it over his desk. "We're going to have many, many dances to make up for the ones we missed that night," he promised, as he took her into his arms.

The music throbbed and the lyrics aroused Dani. Her lips began a tasting tour along Blake's jaw and down his throat where her tongue teased his Adam's apple. Her hands roamed over his back. She tugged his shirt from his hips, unbuttoned it, and stripped it from his shoulders. He pulled his undershirt off to let her hands roam up his chest. She looped her arms around his neck and brought her mouth to his shoulder. Her teeth scrapped seductively over his muscles.

"I want you," she breathed against his skin. "All of you. Forever."

He cradled her in his arms. "Always," he vowed and kissed her so deeply her soul sighed.

An hour later, they lay in each other's arms, their bodies' slick with sweet-lovemaking sweat. When her heart calmed, Dani spoke, "I think I love you more now than I would have if my accident had never happened."

Blake's arms tightened around her. "So do I."

She nestled against him "I want to make dinner for you tomorrow."

"You've made dinner for me plenty of times," he reminded her.

"Not a special dinner. There's going to be wine, music, and candlelight. And I am going to wear a dress." She smiled thinking about the icy-blue dress and matching high heels. She had never worn them before, never had any reason to, but she did now.

"But you can't be late."

"I won't." He kissed her temple. "I promise."

\*\*\*\*

Dani spent all day preparing for the dinner. She set the table with white candles, linen napkins, and silverware. It took her hours to select the music before finally settling on Phil Collins. She poured over the cookbooks she found in his kitchen, scrounged in every cabinet for the ingredients to make her dinner, and slaved in front of the hot stove.

As the peach cobbler baked, she soaked in a bath, bubbles up to her neck, and then slathered on rich cream from toes to earlobes. Back in the kitchen, wearing Blake's robe, she continued to cook. With the steaks marinating in a beer and brown sugar marinade, she did her hair and makeup. She applied a bit of blush to her cheeks, swept mascara over her eyelashes, and smacked on lipstick.

Trying to stay away from the heat, she pan-fried the steaks to a perfect medium-rare, slid them onto white plates, and covered them to keep them warm. She carried all the dishes to the table then hurried upstairs to finish getting ready. She checked her makeup, making sure her mascara hadn't run down her face, spritzed perfume on her wrists and the backs of her knees, slipped on the silk dress, fastened her feet into the two-inch heels, and slung her grandmother's pearls around her neck.

Happy, excited, and feeling beautiful, she descended the stairs and sat at the table to wait for Blake.

## Chapter Ten

The candles had burned down to little stubs of hot wax. The flames flickered. In another minute they'd be out. The steaks were cold and hard. Inside the gravy boat, the gravy had a thick, dark layer of skin over it. The asparagus was wilted, the seasoned and diced new potatoes were shriveled, and the peach cobbler had dried.

With her shoulders hunched over her plate and her temple resting on her fist, she imagined punching Blake the moment she saw him.

The candle closest to her sputtered and died. With a sigh, she bent over, released her screaming feet from the killer heels, and chucked them, one at a time, across the room. Getting up slowly, she looked down at the deep wrinkles in her silk dress. She clenched her teeth as she grabbed the plate with the steaks on them and walked into the kitchen, turning on all the lights as she went.

In the kitchen, she dumped the untouched steaks in the trashcan. On her way back to the dining room, she snatched her jacket off the couch and tugged it on over her dress, hiding the long string of pearls. She continued to the dining room, her bare feet padding on the cold tile. When she picked up the cobbler, wanting to spoon it into the garbage disposal, all the lights went out and the music died.

She looked about blindly. The last time she had looked at the clock, it was just after ten p.m. and the moon was behind a thick layer of snow clouds. She set the cobbler back on the table and made her way across the room using her hands and feet to guide her. After a moment, she found the entrance to the dining room and moved along the wall, searching for the gun Blake always left for her. Her body bumped into the stand and her hands snatched up the gun.

A bang sounded behind her. She spun about, pointing the gun at the front door. Her heart beat against her breast as though it were a punching bag.

*What's happening? Why is the electricity off and what was that noise?* She held her breath in her lungs when she heard the sound of a shotgun being pumped on the other side of the door. She backed away. She knew what a shotgun could do to someone's body; she had seen it many times in the E.R. But, if she had to run, she knew she wouldn't get far. She was bare foot, in a long dress, and couldn't see a damned thing. Her one hope was the gun growing hot in her sweaty grip. If the door opened, she wouldn't run. She would shoot!

She took another step and backed into a solid body. A firm hand clamped over her mouth before she could scream, and a strong arm held her still.

"Don't fight," Blake told her. "The Mob cut the power line. They're outside planning on ambushing the house. My men are in the woods, waiting to ambush them."

She put her hand on his wrist and pulled it from her mouth. "What if they know your men are in the woods," she whispered, "and they have their own men in the woods ready to ambush yours?"

"We have plenty of back up." His words conjured a picture of a blood bath in Dani's mind as he took her hand and pulled her toward the back door. "I need to get you out of here *now*."

Right at that moment, the sliding glass door exploded. Blake shoved her to the floor and covered her with his body. Glass shards showered over them, but Blake didn't waste any time. He jumped to his feet, lifted her over the glass, and rushed her up the stairs where he yanked the attic door open.

She turned to him. He was in all black. Even his forehead, cheeks, and nose were black. He had on green goggles to see in the dark, and weapons up and down his body.

"Go up to the attic and hide," he told her. "Stay there until I come and get you."

She didn't budge.

"What are you waiting for? Go!" She turned to climb up but he forced her around, pulled her close, and kissed her hard. "I don't want to lose you again."

"You won't lose me," she promised.

Their lips collided. It scared her to think this could be the last time they'd kiss, and she hated it felt that way. She let go of Blake, crawled up to the attic, and looked at him over the edge. "Don't you dare get shot."

He gave her a lopsided grin. "Yes, ma'am." He picked up the ladder. "I'll be back for you." Dani nodded and he shut the attic door, casting her into darkness. While she waited for her eyes to adjust, she listened to the gun battle outside. She didn't want to be up there when a war was going on between police officers and mobsters, especially since one of those cops was her man.

She balanced herself on the wooden beams and inched her way to the back of the attic to a little window. She peered out the dusty glass at the sparks below.

*Please, don't let any of those bullets hit Blake*, she prayed. *Please, don't take him away from me. Please—*

The sound of the front door being broken down paralyzed her prayers. Her heart shot up to her throat when she heard heavy boots stomp up the stairs to the second floor.

"I know you're in here, Dani!" Her breath hitched. "And I know your boyfriend is one of those filthy pigs out there." Dani's heart sank like the Titanic. "When I find you, I'll find him."

A loud crash collided against her eardrums. Red and his minnows were ransacking the place while they searched for her. It wouldn't be long before they got smart and headed up to the attic. She lifted up sheets of insulation. Carefully, she braced her hands on the beams and stretched herself between the last two-by-four and the wall. She grabbed a clump of insulation and covered her feet with it. The pink fluff reached her knees when the stampede started up the stairs. She paused, waited for the sound of breaking glass to resume, and draped her thighs with another layer of pink fluff.

They were destroying Blake's room. Glass shattered. She heard loud thuds and splintering wood. She pictured Red kicking open the closet door and flipping the mattress off the bed frame. She lay flat on her back and covered her jittery stomach and aching chest with attic camouflage. The thumps of heavy boots grew louder.

"Dani!" A loud crash sounded. "Dani!" Red's angry voice was beneath the attic. "Dani!"

She took a deep breath before hiding her face in the insulation. As Red pulled down the attic door, she slid her arms beneath her pink blanket. With each thud up the attic steps, her body tensed. Every muscle in her body cramped, her lungs shut down. She held every fiber of her being perfectly still, despite her urge to scratchy her itchy skin.

"Dani!" Red's voice bounced off the walls of the attic. After a moment of silence, the small window above her blew out with a deafening bang. Her spine jerked in fear, but she stayed down.

"She's not up here," Red barked down to his men. "Go outside and start looking for her. Kill every damn police officer you see."

She listened to his retreat down the ladder and the slam of the attic door. Tearing the insulation off her face, she took a deep breath and rubbed her tickling nose. Deep in her nostrils a tornado whirled. She plugged her nose. If she sneezed, she would take the gun in her hand and shoot herself with it. She'd be damned if she let a sneeze get herself killed. Thankfully, the windy storm in her nostrils died. She released her nose, satisfied it wouldn't betray her, and sat up. The thin board beneath her body released a loud creak from its wooden throat. She froze. Even her blood felt like it became ice.

Pink fluff exploded into the air beside her from a shotgun blast. She screamed and sprang onto the two-by-four to see a gaping hole in the middle of the ceiling where she had been lying. The sound of the shotgun being reloaded with shells pushed her out the window.

Her feet sank into the deep snow on the roof and her toes curled. She looked into the night. She was in the backyard and from the sound of the shooting, the battle was out front. She waddled to the edge of the roof and looked over. At five foot nine, she was pretty damn tall for a girl, but the distance between the roof and the ground was more than twice her height. She squatted, gripped the edge in her hands, and flung herself off the roof.

The pearl necklace around her neck flew behind her and caught onto the gutter. It dug into her throat, choking her until the string broke. When she landed in a heap, pearls scattered around her. The wet snow soaked through her dress, staining the expensive silk and pricking her skin with cold needles. She jumped up with a hand to her throat.

The bang of Glocks, explosion of rifles and rapid-fire of semi-automatics grew louder. She was ready to make a dash toward the pocket of woods when a voice made her stop.

"I need a doctor." She whirled. "So I can kill her." Tony London, with his black ponytail, pointed his AK47 at her—the gun with bullets that could go through a cop's vest. She lifted her gun without hesitation. Tony sneered at her. "Shoot me and I'll shoot you." He waved his weapon, mocking her with its size. It was fifty times bigger than hers and a thousand times more deadly.

"Is this the part where I'm supposed to shake and cry and beg you not to kill me?" she said. "Well, that's not going to happen."

"A doctor eager to die? Now that's new."

"A murderer who could've shot me in the back, but

didn't? Now *that's* new. Why didn't you take the shot? Why did you hesitate?"

Tony's grin was ugly. "Maybe I don't want to shoot you."

"Why wouldn't you want to shoot me? Red wants me dead. You all want me dead!"

"Oh, don't get me wrong. I will shoot you. After I take you and have some fun." Tony's eyes gleamed evilly as they roamed over her body.

She swallowed. She knew exactly what he intended to do before killing her. "I'll be more than happy to die after that."

"Then we'll both get what we want." He took a step toward her as her finger lowered on the trigger. A deafening pop exploded in her ear. Tony jolted as a bullet entered his body, but it hadn't come from her gun; hers was on safety.

Tony face planted into the snow and she saw a police officer standing behind him.

"Dani, are you all right?" It was Max, Blake's partner.

"Fine."

*And I'll be even better once I take off the damned safety!*

She flipped the switch and looked back at Max urgently. "Where's Blake? Is he okay?"

"He was the last time I saw him. Now come on, I need to get you the hell out of here!"

She took a few strides, but came to a halt with the sound of bullets being fired. Her breath raced out of her lungs in a puff of white fog when she saw Max crumple to the ground, and a line of smoke rising from Tony's gun.

She raised her gun as Tony aimed his weapon at her. She pulled the trigger twice, releasing two fast bullets. They penetrated his chest and he collapsed into the snow.

Not even bothering to check to make sure he was dead, she yanked up her dress and ran to Max. She fell beside him. "Max. Oh, Max." She took off his vest and put her hand over his chest wound. "You're okay."

But she knew he wasn't. The bullet hole was where his left ribs were. She feared it was lodged in his lung. On its way there, it could've shattered a rib, sending fragments throughout his chest, but there was no telling the full extent of the damage. She couldn't do anything to help him, but she couldn't sit there and do nothing. She couldn't sit there and watch him die. *I'm a doctor damn it!* She ripped a strip of silk off the hem of her dress and pressed it to the wound.

"Dani…go."

She shook her head.

"Dani…" His voice gargled and blood sputtered from his mouth. She wiped it away with another swatch of torn silk. "Between the two of us," he choked out. "I'm going to be the only one dying here."

"Max." She laid a hand on his cheek. "You don't always have to be a gentleman."

Max managed to smile. "I do about this." He inhaled, his body convulsed. She grabbed his hand and held it tight. "Get out of here, Dani. Go!" The boom of a gun made her flinch. "Go." His voice was a bloody croak, but she nodded.

She kissed him goodbye on the cheek. "I love you, Max. Thank you." She sprang to her feet and ran, knowing he probably died before she could take five steps.

Deep in the woods, she ducked behind a thick bush. While she waited, her fingers froze around the gun. She pried her fingers free and slipped the heavy gun into the pocket of her jacket. Feeling sick to her stomach, she hugged her knees to her chest.

Her life had gone from working twenty-four hours straight in the E.R. and saving people's lives to trying desperately to save her own. The Mob aside, her life was finally what she dreamed it could be. All the empty spaces were gone. Her past wasn't a mystery anymore. She had remembered the night of her accident. She remembered Blake. Thinking about him made her heart swell with love and unbearable fear.

*When is this battle going to end?*

Gunshots sounded like bubble wrap being twisted viciously.

*Red wants to kill as many police officers as he can. Each dead officer is his personal victory. Killing Blake will be out of revenge, and killing me will ensure all of his loose ends are taken care of for good.*

A twig snapped and she jumped, her eyes as big as satellites.

"Hello, Dr. Hart." Red stood in front of her, his gun in her face.

"How'd you find me?"

"I followed your footprints in the snow."

"I meant," she growled between clenched teeth, "how did you find me *here*?"

"Well, you're the only Dr. Hart in the area and when we lost you on the streets, I retrieved your cell phone number from your work records. I have many connections and…" He glanced down at his gun. "I can be very persuasive when I want information. I didn't know you were a woman until you answered your cell phone. And I'm very happy you did, because I was able to track you to this neighborhood. I did research to find out the resident's names and followed through with background checks. Imagine my surprise when I saw a picture of one of the residents and recognized him as the same fucking asshole who tried to weasel into my family. And he's a cop to boot. I sent my men to his station to kill him and every pig there, but he was lucky. I called his house the next day and who would answer but Dr. Hart. Two birds, one stone."

Her fingers twitched anxiously. The weight of Blake's gun threatened to tear off her jacket pocket. "Don't even think about it," Red warned. "Take your hand, and the gun, out of the pocket, and don't try anything stupid." She slipped the gun out of her pocket slowly. "Throw it." She chucked it over a bush, out of sight. "Good. Now take off your jacket and put it on the ground." She slipped off the jacket and released it from numb fingers.

In the next instant, Red grabbed her. "Let's go find Officer Herro," he growled in her ear.

Her head whipped back with his sharp tug. The bones in her arm felt like they were being crushed by his grip. To hide her pain, she chomped on the inside of her cheek and started to recite the names of every bone in the body. All two hundred and six of them.

Red yanked her through stabbing thorns and out of the woods. He pulled her past Tony's and Max's bodies where pools of warm blood melted patches of snow. The harsh tug of war continued all the way to the shattered glass door.

She stepped on a large slate of glass, wincing when it cracked beneath her feet, and hopped over the shards.

Red's steel grip steered her past the staircase and straight to the broken front door. The orchestra of guns played on the front lawn and Red pushed her closer to the dangerous music. It was louder at the threshold, as if she was sitting in a front row seat at a concert. Red jostled her, and she stepped into the flashing red and blue lights of a dozen cop cars.

The scene before her was terrifying. Bullet casings speckled the ground like angry confetti. Trails of blood crisscrossed the lawn, and lifeless forms lay here and there. She couldn't see any of their faces, but she prayed none of them were Blake. She could forgive him for missing their dinner date, but she would never forgive him for dying.

When Red forced her out into the open, guns silenced. Eyes smeared in black, eyes behind sniper lenses, eyes dilated from loss of blood, all eyes looked in their direction. Red's breath, hot like a dragon's, blew into her ear. "Call to him."

She shook her head. Red moved the gun from the base of her spine to her temple. "Call to him," he ordered with a sharp jab to the side of her head. She winced. "Now!"

She licked the cold from her lips, but she couldn't. She couldn't call his name. She couldn't call him to his death. A tear of desperation rolled down her cheek.

"Are you crying? Officer Herro, she's crying!" Red laughed hideously. "I think she's scared. Why don't you come to her?" He dug the muzzle deeper into her temple. "Or I can put her out of her misery now."

*Don't come out, Blake. He wants to kill you first.*

*Don't come out. Please, God, don't let him come out.*

A movement caught her attention and her eyes flashed to the right where Blake stepped out of the woods. Her heart plummeted to her stomach. *No!*

"So this is the hero?" Red said it as though he were talking about a cockroach. "Put that big gun down, you don't want to scare Dani anymore than she already is."

Blake held his gun at arm's length, laid it at his feet, and stepped over it. His eyes were on her, and hers were on him. He appeared to be unscathed.

"Keep your hands away from your side firearm and step up onto the porch," Red ordered as he yanked Dani back toward the door. "Don't try anything you'll regret."

Blake stepped onto the porch.

"Good," Red said. "Now come into the house."

Blake stalked forward, his eyes blazing. Red and Dani disappeared into the house and in a couple of steps so did he.

"Close the door," Red ordered.

Blake kicked the door closed. His eyes didn't so much as flinch from Red's.

"We obviously want the same thing." Red stroked Dani's hair. "And boy…" His hand touched her naked shoulder and caressed her arm. "It's beautiful what we want."

Dani's skin crawled. She could feel his eyes on her body and it made her want to scrub herself with bleach. Red's finger skimmed back up her arm. "But she's not the only thing we want, now is it? We want each other dead. Killing each other is the easy part. Deciding who will get her is not. How about we settle this with a good old-fashioned shoot out?" He released the cartridge from his gun, letting it slip to the floor. "One bullet. One shot to kill. What do you say?"

Blake responded by ripping off his Kevlar vest and removing the cartridge of bullets from the Glock waiting at his hip. He lowered it to his side and looked back at Red, his eyes were full of rage and hate.

"Whoever doesn't die will get the prize." The tip of Red's finger skimmed her jaw. She would've jerked her head away if the gun wasn't digging into her temple. "But she's not going to be watching. Oh, no. She's going to be in the middle of it." He shoved Dani forward, causing her to stumble. Trying to stay upright, she felt the gun at the back of her head. "Walk!"

She stepped forward. Her knees wanted to buckle, her legs were gelatin, but she was able to walk until Red ordered her to stop.

"Our only visual is over your pretty shoulders, Doc," Red told her. "So don't move. Don't even flinch."

Dani locked her gaze with Blake, willing him her strength and gathering his around her. His face was as hard as stone. She knew the odds. She knew both of them were going to get shot, and she knew the chances of a lethal wound were great, far greater than survival. With every fiber of her being, every cell in her body, she prayed for Blake to live. He was her high school sweetheart, the man of her dreams. She loved him with all her heart. She mouthed the endearment, wishing she could say it aloud and hoping she'd have a chance to again. She knew Blake understood it, because when he raised his gun, his eyes were fierce.

Horror pumped through her, leaving her ice cold. She couldn't breathe. *What if Blake dies?*

"Don't worry, Doc," Red said from behind her. "This will be over in thirty seconds."

She swallowed hard. Her ears burned red hot. She could feel the two guns, the two sets of eyes trained over her shoulders. Anger sizzled with anticipation. She closed her eyes, held her spine stiff, even when it felt like it would crack. She held her breath, even when she thought her lungs would explode.

She heard a gun go off, followed instantly by another bang. The twin booms echoed in her ears and two bullets sailed past her head as her mind screamed. She opened her eyes to see Blake fall.

"Blake!" She ran to him and fell to her knees. A dark shadow was spreading across his chest. She tore open his uniform. Her hands stilled at the sight of the red stain soaking his white T-shirt.

"How bad is it?"

She looked into Blake's green eyes. "It's not. It's not." She used the hole from the bullet to tear his shirt apart and examined the wound. The bullet was in the middle of his chest. She searched for a puddle of blood at his sides and found none; the bullet was still inside him. She watched blood bubble out of the wound and pressed his shirt to it, while praying his artery hadn't been clipped.

"Red?" Blake asked.

She peered over her shoulder. Red was flat on his back in a thick pool of blood. "He's down, doesn't appear to be breathing. I don't want to leave you to go check, though."

She turned back to find Blake's eyes shut. "Blake?" She put a cold hand to his cheek. To her relief, his eyelids opened. "I need you to keep your eyes open, okay?"

"Sure. You sound scared."

"Of course I am, you idiot. I told you not to get shot. If you weren't already injured, I'd kick your ass."

He wore a lopsided grin on his pale face. "You could always kick my ass later."

"I plan on it."

His lips spread into a smile. "I look forward to it."

Dread sliced through her heart.

"Dani, I want to…" His face contorted and a strangled sound stumbled out of his throat.

"Blake, what is it?" He grabbed her as his body convulsed. A sea of blood rushed over her hands. "No. Oh God, no, don't do this."

His eyes glazed over, all color drained from his face. His chest rose and fell quickly beneath her palms.

"Dani…I love you."

She shook her head. "Don't you dare." But his eyes were already closing. "Blake?" He didn't respond. She grabbed the radio from his hip. "Officer down! Blake is hit. I need an ambulance now!"

Chief Witten's voice came through the radio. "The paramedics are coming."

She laid her hand against Blake's neck and felt his pulse fade.

## Chapter Eleven

Blake was hooked up to a heart monitor, an oxygen cannula, an IV bag, and practically everything else in the hospital. Dani sat at his bedside with her hand over his. She had been with him for three long days and even longer nights in the Intensive Care Unit, waiting for him to regain consciousness.

"Blake." Her voice cracked. She tried to swallow her tears, but they clogged her throat. "Please wake up. I refuse to live without you."

This time, they had opposite roles. This time, it was him in the hospital bed, not her. "I love you, Blake." Fresh tears slipped from her eyes. "Please wake up, I love you."

She watched him. As minutes slowly passed on the wall clock and his eyes remained closed, more tears filled her own. Her eyelids lowered, squeezing hot tears between her lashes. They flowed down her cheeks.

She dropped her head onto the edge of his bed and cried.

*God, don't do this to us again,* she pleaded. *I love him so much. Please wake him. Please.*

She listened to the heart monitor. Each beep broke her heart even more. *He's alive, but I need him awake. God, I need him!* She took a shuddering breath as oxygen flowed from the tank beside her, through the thin tubes around his ears and into his nostrils.

*Please bring him back to me. I want to see his beautiful green eyes again. Let me see them. Wake him up. Please wake him. Please God...*

"Dani?"

She shot to her feet, a hand to her chest. She stared down at him, but his eyes were sealed. "Blake?" She pressed a hand to her mouth to quiet her gasp when his eyelids drifted open. A sob hit her palm.

"Are you really awake?" she asked, afraid her eyes were deceiving her, that she was dreaming this, imagining this, but the corner of his mouth titled up.

"I love you. I love you so much!" She kissed his forehead and cheeks as her tears spilled onto his face. She pulled back to look into his evergreen eyes. "Please tell me you remember who I am."

He lifted his hand, with the intravenous line in it, and touched the side of her face. "I could never forget you, Dani."

She kissed him. "You scared me. You really scared me."

He wiped away her tears. "I'm sorry, but you know I had to do it. There was nothing else I could've done to save you. To save us."

"I know. You're my hero."

He lifted her hand to his lips. "Thanks. Now can you get my pants for me?"

She put a hand on her hip. "You're not leaving the hospital today."

"I figured that. Can you get them anyway? There's something in my right pocket."

She opened the cabinet and pulled out the bag where his pants and other items were being stored. She moved back to the bed as she dug her hand into the pocket. When she felt what was there, her gaze flew to his.

"Take it out," he coaxed.

Her heart hammered in her chest. She pulled her hand out and looked down at the small velvet box.

"Marry me, Dani."

She swallowed. "Should you be asking me this now? You're on some serious drugs."

He smiled at the IV hanging above him. "They're working, too, but I bought the ring the morning your memory came back."

She stared at him in shock. "Why didn't you ask me then?"

"Because I wanted to ask you after I got Red."

"But I would've said yes if you had."

He lifted a brow. "Will you say yes now?"

"I don't know." She took the ring out of its case and gave it to him. "Ask me."

He took the ring and her hand. "You were the first girl I ever loved, Elle. And you're going to be the last. I want to make up for what we've lost. I want to love you for the rest of our lives. I'm thinking another eighty years or more."

She smiled. "I'll hold you to it."

He smiled, too. "Danielle Hart, will you marry me?"

She pressed her lips to his. "Yes." He slipped the diamond on her finger and she examined it. "Dr. Hart-Herro. Has a nice *ring* to it."

Blake frowned. "Hyphenate? I thought you said my wife would be proud to have my name?"

"I am proud," she said, "which is why I want it right next to my maiden name. Right next to Hart, because you have my heart."

Blake kissed her finger right above the ring he gave her. "So when do you want to get married?"

Epilogue

Blake stood at a candle-lit altar watching Dani walk toward him. She wore a sleek red dress. It flowed down her hips into a long, sweeping train. Her red hair was in an elegant bun with a sparkling diamond tiara on top. In a matter of minutes, she would become his wife.

She took her place beside him and reached for his hands. He said his vows, vows with his favorite lyrics to rock songs twined with his promises. When it was time for them to kiss, he snatched her, looped her around, and gave her an elaborate kiss. The church filled with whistles and laughter.

At the reception, he danced with her to "I Don't Want to Miss a Thing" by Aerosmith and when the song ended she whispered in his ear, "Now that we are husband and wife, what do you think about being a daddy?"

\*\*\*\*

Seven months later, Dani gave birth to a baby boy they named Jarred. Blake cuddled his son in his arms and gazed down at him with a big, proud smile.

"It only took me thirty seconds after your mom said she was pregnant for me to fall in love with you," he said and looked at his wife. "You're my hero, Dani."

She smiled groggily at him. "And you're my heart."

## A word about the author...

Chrys Fey is a lover of rock music just like Dani Hart in *30 Seconds*. Whenever she's writing at her desk, headphones are always emitting the sounds of her musical muses -especially that of her favorite band, 30 Seconds to Mars, the inspiration behind the title.

*30 Seconds* is her second eBook with The Wild Rose Press. Her debut, *Hurricane Crimes*, is also available on Amazon.

Discover her writing tips at:

www.writewithfey.blogspot.com

And connect with her on Facebook:

www.facebook.com/ChrysFey

She loves to get to know her readers!

Also available from The Wild Rose Press, Inc.

30 Seconds Before
*Prequel to 30 Seconds*
by Chrys Fey

Blake Herro is a cop in the Cleveland Police Force. Ever since he was a child, he wanted to do right by the city he loved by cleaning up the streets and protecting its citizens. Red, a notorious mobster, has other plans.

On a bitter December night, ten police officers are drawn into a trap and killed by Red's followers. Blake wants to bring down the Mob to avenge his fallen brothers and to prevent other cops from being murdered. Except the only way he can do that is by infiltrating the Mob.

Every minute he's with these mobsters he's in danger. Around every corner lies the threat of coming face to face with a gun. Will he make it out of the Mob alive, or will he be their next victim?

*****

Hurricane Crimes
by Chrys Fey

After her car breaks down, Beth Kennedy is forced to stay in Florida, the target of Hurricane Sabrina. She stocks up supplies, boards up windows, and hunkers down to wait out the storm, but her plan unravels when she witnesses a car accident. Risking her life, she braves the winds to save the driver. Just when she believes they are safe, she finds out the man she saved could possibly be more dangerous than the severe weather.

Donovan Goldwyn only wanted to hide from the police, but the hurricane shoved his car into a tree. Now he's trapped with a beautiful woman while the evidence that can prove his innocence to a brutal crime is out there for anyone to find.

As Hurricane Sabrina wreaks havoc, Beth has no other choice but to trust Donovan to stay alive. But will she survive, or will she become another hurricane crime?

Thank you for purchasing
this publication of The Wild Rose Press, Inc.

For questions or more information
contact us at
info@thewildrosepress.com.

The Wild Rose Press, Inc.
www.thewildrosepress.com

To visit with authors of
The Wild Rose Press, Inc.
join our yahoo loop at
http://groups.yahoo.com/group/thewildrosepress/